"What could be so terrible that a child would stop speaking?"

Sophie asked. "I can't imagine."

Something flickered in Kade's stolid expression, a twitch of muscle, the narrowing of coffee-colored eyes in a hard face. "I plan to find out," he said.

"Your police experience should help us find Davey's family," Sophie said.

"Us?"

"Well…" She'd been there when Davey was found and she didn't intend to walk away and leave him with all these unanswered questions. "I know the community really well. People trust me. They'll talk to me. I don't know the first thing about investigating a missing boy." She stopped, frowned. Davey wasn't missing exactly. "Or rather, a found boy. But I know how to deal with people."

Kade raised a palm. "Let's not get ahead of ourselves. It's early yet. Someone may come home from work tonight, find their son gone, and call in. Problem solved."

"Do you think they will?" she asked hopefully.

"To be honest?" He dropped his arms to his sides, shot a look toward the living room. "No."

Something in the sudden clip of his voice chilled Sophie's bones.

Books by Linda Goodnight

Love Inspired

LINDA GOODNIGHT

Winner of a RITA® Award for excellence in inspirational fiction, Linda Goodnight has also won a Booksellers' Best, an ACFW Book of the Year and a Reviewers' Choice Award from *RT Book Reviews*. Linda has appeared on the Christian bestseller list and her romance novels have been translated into more than a dozen languages. Active in orphan ministry, this former nurse and teacher enjoys writing fiction that carries a message of hope and light in a sometimes dark world. She and her husband, Gene, live in Oklahoma. Readers can write to her at linda@lindagoodnight.com, or c/o Love Inspired Books, 233 Broadway, Suite 1001, New York, NY 10279.

The Christmas Child
Linda Goodnight

Love Inspired

Recycling programs for this product may not exist in your area.

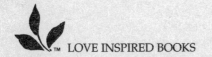

LOVE INSPIRED BOOKS

ISBN-13: 978-0-373-81575-3

THE CHRISTMAS CHILD

Copyright © 2011 by Linda Goodnight

www.LoveInspiredBooks.com

Printed in U.S.A.

For Diane in Dallas, who makes me laugh and cheers me on, as well as all you other dependable, wonderful readers. You know who you are—and I treasure each of you. Thank you for your letters and emails, your Facebook messages and blog comments. This book is for you!

Chapter One

In twenty years of Dumpster diving, Popbottle Jones had found his share of surprises in other people's trash. But nothing prepared him for what he discovered one chilly November dawn.

Agile as a monkey at seventy-two, Popbottle hopped over the side of the giant bin located downwind of Redemption's municipal building and dropped lightly onto a mound of battered cardboard boxes. The usual garbage and old-food smells rose to greet him, odors he'd trained his nose to ignore in pursuit of more profitable treasures. After all, he and his business partner, GI Jack, were in the recycling business.

From one corner of the dimly lit bin came a scratching sound. His heart sank. Rats or kittens, he suspected. Rats he shooed. The kittens, though, troubled him. He'd never leave domestic creatures to be scooped into a compactor and bulldozed at a landfill.

Gingerly picking his way through the mess, Popbottle directed his steps and his miner's lamp toward the sound. His stomach plummeted. Not rats. Not kittens, though two eyes stared out. Blue eyes. Frightened eyes. The eyes of a child.

Taking a bullet would have been easier, cleaner, quicker. Dying slowly wasted a lot of time.

Kade McKendrick dropped one hand to the golden retriever sitting patiently beside him along the riverbank and tried to relax.

Even now, when he'd been shipped off to Redemption, Oklahoma, for R & R, he wielded a fishing rod like a weapon, fingers tight on the reel's trigger. He'd become too paranoid to go anywhere unarmed.

Memories swamped him. Faces swam up from the muddy red river to accuse. Kade shifted his gaze to the far bank where straggling pale brown weeds poked up from the early winter landscape, hopeless sprouts with nothing in their future but more of the same. Feathery frost tipped the dead grass, shiny in the breaking dawn.

"Might as well give it up, Sheba." Kade reeled in the ten-pound test line, mocking his ambitious tackle. The clerk at the bait and tackle warned him that fish weren't biting this time of year.

He slammed the metal tackle box, startling the dog and a red-tailed hawk still napping on a nearby branch. The bird took flight, wings flapping like billows over the calm, cold waters. Sheba looked on, quivering with intense longing. Together, man and dog watched the hawk soar with lazy grace toward the rising sun. Other than a rare car passing on the bridge, all was quiet and peaceful here on the predawn river. The place drew him like a two-ton magnet in those dark hours when sleep, the vicious tease, evaded him.

Kade sniffed. His nose was cold, but the morning air, with crisp, clean sharpness, invigorated more than chilled. He picked up the scent of someone's fireplace, a cozy home, he surmised, with two-point-five kids, a Betty Crocker mom and a dad who rose early to feed the fire with fragrant hickory wood.

His lip curled, cynic that he was. Happy ever after was a Hallmark movie.

He, too, had risen early, but not for a cozy fire and a loving family. Although gritty-eyed with fatigue, he hadn't slept a full eight hours in months. But the shrink said he was making progress.

Kade huffed, breath a gray cloud. The shrink probably didn't wake up when his dog barked.

Gathering his gear, Kade started toward his car, a red Mazda Miata parked at an angle near the edge of the Redemption River Bridge. Sheba padded softly at his side, a loyal, undemanding companion who never complained about the nocturnal ramblings.

His great-aunt, on the other hand...

Ida June rose early and she'd be waiting for his return, spouting sluggard quotes, her favorite being, "The field of the sluggard is overtaken by weeds." There were no weeds in Aunt Ida June's fields. One positive aspect of visiting his feisty great-aunt was that she kept him too busy all day to think. Days were all right. Nights were killing him.

Sophie Bartholomew bebopped out the door of the *Redemption Register,* a happy tune on her lips and an order for six dozen cookies on her notepad. She stopped on the sidewalk and danced a little boogie to celebrate the sale. Her students would be pumped, too.

Sophie loved mornings, especially this time of year with Christmas right around the corner. Already, Redemption geared up for the monthlong celebration.

This crisp morning when the town was just awakening, the scent of fresh doughnuts tantalized the streets in front of the Sugar Shack bakery and café. Sophie headed there next to round up more orders for the annual fifth-grade charity cookie sale. Miriam, owner of the Sugar Shack, never minded, even though the sales cut into her business.

Down the block a city worker dangled from a

bucket truck to lace white lights along the front of the town's historic bank building. Sophie gave a little wave. Christmas was unofficially here, and no one was happier about that than Sophie.

She loved everything about Christmas, from the celebrations and festivities to church and decorated cookies and gaily wrapped gifts. Even the commercialism didn't bother her. Christmas, she'd long ago decided, meant joy and love and Jesus, in whatever form it was celebrated.

Across the street on the town square, Ida June Click, octogenarian handywoman, pounded on a half-erected stable while a lean, dark man unloaded lumber from a truck, his navy plaid shirt open over a white T-shirt. Sophia recognized him as Kade McKendrick, Ida June's nephew, although Sophie didn't know him well. He was new in town, but her single friends and several not-so-singles noticed his comings and goings. He mostly stayed to himself. His quiet aloofness made everyone wonder, including her. But he was a looker, as her close friend Jilly Fairmont said. A mysterious looker. What could be more intriguing to a female? Not that Sophie thought all that much about her single status. She was too busy teaching kids and loving the life the Lord had given her.

She had one hand on the glass door of the Sugar Shack when she heard a shout. Over on the curb by the buff-brick municipal building, GI Jack, the eccentric old Dumpster diver who ran a recycling business and created junk art, waved his arms and yelled for help.

"Ida June," he called to the twig of woman in bright red overalls and a man's work jacket. "Get over here quick."

"Here" was a spot right next to an industrial-size trash bin.

"Not another cat. My cup runneth over already." But the feisty eightysomething woman hustled toward him just the same.

So did Sophie. GI Jack was not an alarmist, and one quick glance told her Popbottle Jones, the other eccentric Dumpster diver, was nowhere to be seen.

Traffic was slow this time of day, and Sophie darted across the street with barely a glance. Had something happened to Popbottle Jones?

"What can we do? Shall we call for an ambulance? I have my cell phone." Ida June, still a little breathless from the jog, whipped a modern smartphone from the bib of her overalls. "We must get him out of that Dumpster ASAP. He who hesitates is lost."

Confusion clouded GI Jack's face. "Well, yes, ma'am, I reckon so, but we don't need no ambulance."

"If Popbottle is hurt—"

The funny old man blinked. "Popbottle ain't hurt."

"My friend is correct. I've suffered no ill effect."

Ulysses E. "Popbottle" Jones grasped the top of the heavy metal trash bin and peered over the edge, his red miner's hat tipped to one eye. "But we do require assistance."

Curiosity got the better of Sophie and she tiptoed up for a look. The sight she beheld chipped off a piece of her teacher's heart. Cowering against the side of the bin and surrounded by trash, a young boy, maybe eight or nine, clutched a book against his chest and stared out with round blue eyes. Poorly dressed for the cold day, his shaggy blond hair hung limp and dirty around a pale, thin face smeared with something yellow, probably mustard from the piece of old hamburger gripped in his other hand.

"The small fellow won't allow me near him," Popbottle said with some chagrin as he hopped to the street. "Must be my unusual attire or perhaps the miner's lamp. I thought one of you ladies would fare better."

"Probably thought you were an alien from Jupiter," Ida June grumbled. Barely tall enough to see inside, she chinned herself like a gymnast, peered in, then slithered back to earth, muttering. "My nephew will know what to do." Whirling toward the town square she barked loud enough to be heard over the din of a city truck rattling past. "Kade, on the double! We need help."

Sophie, too concerned with the child to wait, said, "GI, boost me up."

The gentle old man, still strong as the soldier he'd been, patted his bent knee. "Foot here."

She grabbed the top of the trash bin and vaulted up and in to slide unceremoniously onto a pile of damp newspapers. She rested there for a few seconds to study the little boy and gauge his reaction to her presence. Dampness soaked through the back of her sweater. She'd need a trip home before schooltime. Not that her clothes mattered at the moment.

When the little boy didn't scramble away, she slowly moved toward him, picking her way across the junk, careful not to turn an ankle in the heeled boots.

"Hello, there," she said in her kindest voice. "My name is Sophie. What's your name?"

The question was met with a silent stare.

Sophie went into a crouch, inches from the child, but careful not to touch until he was ready. Holding back was hard. She was a toucher, a hugger, believing children needed physical connection. "I'm a nice person, honey. You can talk to me and I'll help you."

Still only that bleak stare.

"I'm a teacher here in Redemption. Fifth grade. What grade are you in?"

Nothing.

Outside the trash bin voices rose and fell—Ida June's spit and vinegar, and a chorus of males. By now, someone had likely called the police station, and Sophie worried the sight of an officer might frighten the boy even more. He was like a wary, wild thing, cornered and ready to bolt at the first opportunity.

Metal scraped against the outer bin. Someone else was scrambling up the side. The boy's gaze shifted to a spot behind Sophie just as that someone dropped to the surface with catlike quiet.

Sophie glanced over one shoulder to see the trim, lithe, dark-as-a-shadow nephew of Ida June Click. His eyes, the same espresso brown as his hair, met hers in a narrow squint. There was something lethal about Kade McKendrick, and she remembered the rumor that he'd been a big-city cop or in the DEA or some such. He looked more like a man who'd been on the wrong side of the law than a police officer.

"The cookie lady," he said with an unsmiling nod.

Sophie offered a cheeky grin. "You'll order some yet. It's a great cause." Every year she and her fifth graders baked and sold Christmas cookies and contributed the proceeds to charity.

He went to his heels beside her and hitched his chin toward the child. In the bin, large as it was, three was a crowd. "Who's your friend?"

She tilted her face toward his, noticed the tense lines around his eyes and mouth. "One frightened boy."

Kade turned a quiet look on the child. "Hey, buddy, what's your name?"

Sophie waited, but when the child's response was more silence, she said, "He's not said a word to me, either."

"What's that he's holding?" Kade gestured, stirring the scent of warm, working male and clean cotton shirt, a welcome respite from the stink of trash.

"A book."

"Good work, Sherlock," he said, lightly enough that Sophie would have laughed if she hadn't been so concerned for the child. "What kind of book and why is he gripping it like a lifeline?"

Sophie wondered the same thing.

To the boy, she said, "I'm a teacher, honey. I love books. What kind of story are you reading?"

He shifted slightly, his gaze flickering to the oversize book.

"Will you show it to me? Maybe we can read it together over breakfast? Are you hungry?" She extended an upturned palm and waited. She was surprisingly aware of Kade squatted in the trash next to her. She knew little about him, other than rumors and that he was good-looking in a black panther kind of way. An interesting energy simmered, in this of all places, as his arm brushed hers.

She ignored the sensation and smiled encouragement at the little boy, all the while praying for guidance and a way to connect.

Slowly, with stark hope and a dose of anxiety, the towheaded boy relinquished the picture book.

Sophie shifted nearer, relaxing some and moving easily into teacher mode. She knew books, knew kids, knew how to relate.

"This is beautiful." She touched the brightly colored cover. "Is it your favorite?"

For the first time, the boy responded. His head bobbed up and down. He scooted closer and opened the cover of the popular Christmas tale. Sophie shot a glance at Kade, who offered a quick, approving hitch of his chin. For some reason, his encouragement pleased her. Not that she wanted to impress Ida June's great-nephew, but they *were* in this crowded Dumpster together. The thought made her giggle. The males gave her identical, bewildered looks.

"Look what we have here," Sophie said, her finger on the flyleaf inscription. "*To Davey. Happy Birthday. Love, Mama.* You must be Davey."

Eagerly, the child nodded, his face lighting up.

Someone rapped sharply on the side of the trash bin. The sound echoed like a metallic gong. Davey jumped, then shrank back into himself.

"Are you two taking up residence in there?"

Sophie glanced up. Three pairs of eyes peered back from above the edge, watching the scene below.

"Ida June has the patience of a housefly," Kade muttered, but rose and offered a hand to the little boy. "Come on, Davey, I'm hungry. Let's get some pancakes."

Davey hesitated only a moment before putting his small hand in Kade's much larger one. Then, with eyes wide and unsure, he reached for Sophie on the other side. Body tense, his fingers trembled. Over his head, Kade and Sophie exchanged glances. She wasn't sure what she expected from Kade McKendrick, but anger burned from eyes dark with a devastation she couldn't understand.

In that one look, Sophie received a stunning message. Davey was lost and alone. So was Kade McKendrick.

Chapter Two

❧

Davey sat in Police Chief Jesse Rainmaker's desk chair, swiveling back and forth, while the adults—Sophie, Ida June and Kade—discussed his situation. The Dumpster divers had come and gone, promising to "spread the word" and find where Davey belonged.

Kade hoped they could, but he wasn't holding his breath. He'd seen this before, although finding a kid in a trash can was a new low. A kid, tossed away like tissue. Use once and discard. Yeah, he'd seen plenty of that. Only they got used more than once before they ran or were discarded.

Kade's gut burned with the implication. He hoped he was wrong. He turned his back to the sad little scene and perused the faxes and photos on a bulletin board. Creeps, losers, scum. Somebody somewhere knew who this kid was and what had happened to him.

"Has he told you anything at all? Where he's from, his name, his parents. Anything?" Police Chief Jesse Rainmaker was a solid man. In a few short weeks, Kade had come to respect the understaffed officer and his handful of deputies. They were small-town but efficient and smart. Good cops.

"Nothing," Sophie said. "Even over breakfast, he didn't say a word. I'm starting to wonder if he can speak."

The sweet-faced schoolteacher had drawn a chair up next to Davey. She was good with the kid, calmed him, gave him a sense of security. For a fraction of a minute in the Dumpster, she'd done the same for him. It was a weird feeling.

Kade pivoted. "Why don't we ask him? Obviously, he can hear."

"Or he reads lips," Sophie said.

Chief Rainmaker tilted his head. "Hadn't thought of that."

"I know sign language. I can try that, too," Sophie said, moving round in front of Davey. "Davey."

The dirty little boy focused on her face. Some of his fear had dissipated, but he remained edgy, watchful, uncertain.

With a grace Kade found beautiful, the woman moved her hands in silent communication. Davey stared but didn't respond.

"Well, that didn't work. Davey, can you hear me?"

An eager head bob.

"Why won't you talk to me?"

Davey shrugged, one hand moving to his throat.

"Let's send him over to the clinic," Rainmaker said. "Have him checked out. Either he won't talk for some reason or he can't."

Restless in the small office Kade paced from the bulletin board to the boy and back again. Someone had put an automatic air freshener on top of the file cabinet to counteract the smell of burned coffee and stale shoes. Every few minutes, a spurt of fragrance hissed a girly scent into the air. Jesse either had a wife or secretary. No self-respecting cop would buy—Kade squinted at the can—white tea and roses. Smelled pretty good, though.

"Then what happens to him?" he asked.

Rainmaker rounded his desk, a long metal structure overflowing with paperwork. Kade empathized. Paperwork was the bane of cops.

The chief shuffled through some messages, pulled a stack of faxes from the basket. "Nothing on the wires about a missing child in the area, but I'll make more calls and get the word out. We'll hear something soon."

Kade didn't let it go. Couldn't. "If you don't?"

"Child protective services will take over. I'll have to notify them anyway. Someone is responsible for letting this boy get in this situation. Finding them is my job. Taking care of the child isn't."

Kade grunted. Shoulders tense, he shoved his

hands into the pockets of his leather jacket. He'd told himself the same thing once. It was a lie. Taking care of the kids was everyone's job.

Ida June, who'd remained amazingly silent for a full ten minutes, piped up in her take-no-guff tone. "We'll take the boy home with us. No need to call anyone."

His aunt's idea took Kade by surprise, but he didn't object. He wanted to keep an eye on Davey, just as he wanted to find out who'd left him in such a condition. Someone needed to pay big-time. And Kade was in the mood to be the collector.

"Now, Miss Ida June, you know I have to follow the law," Jesse said patiently.

"Please, Jesse," Sophie said, voice as sweet as her face. "I'd take him myself, but I have to get to school. I'm already late and an aide is watching my class, but Davey's too fragile to go with another stranger right now."

If Rainmaker could resist that face and tone, he was a strong man.

"Girl's right," Ida June announced with a slap to the desktop. Davey jumped, blue eyes blinking rapidly. Sophie placed a soothing hand on his knee. "We'll take Davey to the clinic, me and my nephew here, and then home to clean up. I figure the little man is tuckered plum out. He can rest up for a few hours at my place, and then if you haven't found his mama and daddy, you can call Howard Prichard."

Jesse rubbed the back of his neck. "Tell you what, Miss Ida June, I'll give Howard a call and apprise him of the situation. If he agrees, it's a deal."

Good luck with that, Kade thought.

"Well, get to it." Ida June crossed her arms over the front of her overalls. "Time wasted is gone forever and Lord knows, at my age, I can't afford to lose any."

Mouth twitching, Jesse made the phone call. When the social worker agreed with Ida June's plan, Kade was amazed. Small towns worked differently than the city where the letter of the law was followed, regardless. Here, apparently, human beings took precedence over protocol. Interesting.

They prepared to load Davey and his book into Kade's truck. Ida June had wanted him to ride with her, but Kade and Jesse both said, "No!" with such force that Ida June puffed up like an adder and stalked off. *Kade* didn't ride with her. He sure wasn't putting a child in the truck with her.

"She cut across the street yesterday, slapped a U-turn as if there weren't cars coming both ways, all because there was a parking spot on the other side."

Rainmaker nodded sagely. "I think she got her driver's license out of a cereal box."

Kade arched an eyebrow. "She has one?"

Both men chuckled.

"Come on, Davey," Kade said, taking the boy by the hand.

Davey hopped obediently from the chair and reached for Sophie. Her face crumbled. "Oh, honey, I can't go with you. I have to go to work."

Davey wrenched away from Kade to throw both arms around Sophie's middle. With a helpless look toward Kade, she hugged Davey close against a long blue sweater. Kade got a funny kick in the gut and fought off the urge to join the hug fest.

"You'll come to the house after school." His was a statement, not a question. He knew she'd come.

She nodded, gray eyes distressed. "I'll be there right after three." She held Davey back from her a little, hands on his shoulders. "Do you hear me, Davey? Go with Kade to Miss Ida June's house. They'll take good care of you, and as soon as school is out, I'll be there. We'll read your book as many times as you want. Okay?"

Looking from her to Kade and back as if he thought the pair of them went together, Davey thought over the proposition. Then, he retrieved the book he'd dropped, clasped Kade's hand and followed him to the truck.

Sophie's school day started out shaky, but she, an eternal optimist, was certain things would get better. They didn't.

After rushing home for a quick clothing change

she arrived to find her class in chaos. Emily Baker had suffered a seizure and had to go to the hospital. Even though everyone knew about Emily's disorder, witnessing a seizure frightened the class. Even Zoey Bowman, the vet's daughter whose blindness only increased her compassion and wisdom, had not known how to react. She and best friend, blonde and bouncy Delaney Markham, huddled together holding hands, desks scooted close.

By the time Sophie settled the group down with assurances that Emily was not going to die and a promise to get Mrs. Baker on the speakerphone in a few hours so they all could hear an update for themselves, lunchtime arrived.

"Academics took a backseat this morning," Carmen, the teacher's aide, said as she slid her lunch tray onto the cafeteria table next to Sophie. A fortysomething bleached blonde with an extra twenty pounds, Carmen floated between classrooms doing whatever was needed.

"Caring for people is more important sometimes," Sophie said. She sniffed a forkful of mystery casserole, a combination of tomato and meat scent with sticky pasta in the mix. Or was that rice?

"Don't say that to Mr. Gruber."

"I already have." Sophie jabbed a fork into the glob and took a bite. Not bad. Not good. She reached for the salt and pepper.

"Only you could get away with talking like that to the principal."

"Oh, that's not true. He's fair to everyone. Here, try salt on that." She offered the shakers to her seatmate.

"Anything to hide the taste," Carmen said with a wry grin.

The clatter and din of kids in a cafeteria made talking tough, but Carmen had the kind of voice that could be heard by thirty rowdy kids in a noisy gym. "Come on, Sophie, everyone knows Mr. Gruber has a thing for you."

"Shh. Not so loud." Sophie glanced around, hoping no one had heard. Carmen chuckled, the sound of a woman who enjoyed teasing and gossip, not necessarily in that order. Biff Gruber was a decent man and a good, if uptight, principal. Sophie respected his leadership.

She scooped another bite of the bland casserole, eyeing it suspiciously. "What is this anyway?"

Carmen laughed at the common refrain as the glass double doors swept open. Noise gushed in like a sudden wind. A flurry of overzealous teens, shuffling their feet and jockeying for position in line, pushed inside. Over the din, Carmen said, "There's your dad."

Sophie glanced up. Amid the gangly teens, a graying man in white dress shirt and yellow cartoon tie grinned at something one of his students said.

"Oh, good. I was hoping he'd stop for lunch today." Her dad taught science in the high school. Many days he ate at his desk while tutoring kids. She raised a hand, flagged him over to join them.

As his gray plastic tray scraped onto the table across from her and he greeted the other teachers with an easy smile, the familiar pang of fierce love stirred in Sophie's chest. Mark Bartholomew had aged more than the five years since his divorce from Sophie's mother, a divorce he'd never wanted. Worse, Meg Bartholomew had remarried almost immediately. The implication of an affair still stung, a bitter, unexpected betrayal. Sophie could only imagine how humiliated and hurt her father must have felt.

"Hi, Dad. How's your day?"

"Better now that I see your smiling face. How is yours?" He spread a narrow paper napkin on his lap and tucked in his "mad scientist" tie.

"Something crazy happened this morning."

Expression comical, he tilted his head, prematurely graying hair glossy beneath the fluorescent lights. "Crazier than usual? This is a school, remember? The holiday season always stirs up the troops."

Sophie and her father shared this love of teaching and the special hum of energy several hundred kids brought into a building. At Christmas, the energy skyrocketed.

"We found a lost boy in the municipal Dumpster."

Her father lowered his fork, frowning, as she repeated the morning's events. When she finished, he said, "That's tragic, honey. Anything I can do?"

"Pray for him. Pray for Chief Rainmaker to find his family." She shrugged. "Just pray."

He patted the back of her hand. "You got it. Don't get your heart broken."

"Dad," she said gently.

"I know you. You'll get involved up to your ears. Sometimes your heart's too big."

"I take after my dad."

The statement pleased him. He dug into the mystery casserole. "What is this?"

Sophie giggled as she and Carmen exchanged glances. "Inquiring minds want to know."

He chewed, swallowed. "Better than an old bachelor's cooking."

He said the words naturally, without rancor, but Sophie ached for him just the same. Dad alone in their family home without Mom unbalanced the world. Even though Sophie had offered to give up her own place and move in with him, her father had resisted, claiming he wanted his "bachelor pad" all to himself. Sophie knew better. He'd refused for her sake, worried she'd focus on his life instead of hers.

Carmen dug an elbow into Sophie's side. "Mr. Gruber just came in."

"Principals eat, too."

Carmen rolled her eyes. "He's headed this direction."

Sophie's father looked from one woman to the other. "Have I missed something?"

"Nothing, Dad. Pay no mind to Carmen. She's having pre-Christmas fantasies."

"Mr. Gruber is interested in your daughter."

"Carmen! Please. He is not." She didn't want him to be. A picture of the quietly intense face of Kade McKendrick flashed in her head. This morning's encounter had stirred more than her concern for a lost child.

"Gruber's a good man," her dad said. He stopped a moment to turn to the side and point at a pimply boy for throwing a napkin wad. The kid grinned sheepishly, retrieved the wad and sat down. The high schoolers were convinced Mr. Bartholomew had eyes in the back of his head.

"Dad, do not encourage rumors."

Her father lifted both hands in surrender as the principal arrived at their table. Biff Gruber nodded to those gathered, then leaned low next to Sophie's ear. His blue tie sailed dangerously close to the mystery casserole. Sophie suppressed a giggle.

"I need to see you in my office, please. During your plan time is fine."

Without another word, he walked away.

"So much for your romantic theories," Sophie told a wide-eyed Carmen. "That did not sound like an interested man."

"No kidding. Wonder what he wants," Carmen said, watching the principal exit the room. "An ultimatum like that can't be good."

Sophie put aside her fork. "Sure it can. Maybe he wants to order ten-dozen cookies."

Carmen looked toward the ceiling with a sigh. "You'd put a positive spin on it if he fired you."

Well, she'd try. But she couldn't help wondering why her principal had been so abrupt.

She found out two hours later, seated in his tidy, narrow office. The space smelled of men's cologne and the new leather chair behind the unusually neat, polished mahogany desk. It was a smell, she knew, that struck terror in the hearts of sixth-grade boys. A plaque hung on the wall above Biff Gruber's head as warning to all who entered: Attitudes Adjusted While You Wait.

"I understand you're doing the cookie project again this year," he said without preliminary.

Sophie brightened. Maybe he *did* want to place an order. She folded her hands in her lap, relaxed and confident. This was Biff and she was not a sixth-grade rowdy. "I turned in the lesson plan last week. We're off to a promising start already and I hope to raise even more money this year."

Biff positioned his elbows on the desk and bounced his fingertips together. The cuffs of his crisply ironed shirt bobbed up and down against his pale-haired wrists. The light above winked on a silver watch. His expression, usually open and friendly, remained tight and professional. Sophie's hope for a cookie sale dissipated.

"We've had some complaints from parents," he said.

Sophie straightened, the news a complete surprise. No one had ever complained. "About the project? What kind of complaints? Students look forward to this event from the time they're in second and third grade."

In fact, kids begged to participate. Other classes loitered in her doorway, volunteered and occasionally even took orders for her. This project was beloved by all. Wasn't it?

"How many years have you been doing this, Sophie?" The principal's tone was stiff, professional and uneasy.

Suddenly, she felt like one of the students called into the principal's office for making a bad judgment. At the risk of sounding defensive, she said, "This is year five. Last year we donated the proceeds, a very nice amount, I might add, to the local women's shelter. Afterward, Cheyenne Bowman spoke to our class and even volunteered to teach a self-protection seminar to the high-school girls."

Biff, however, had not followed up on that offer from the shelter's director, a former police officer and assault victim.

"I'm aware the project does a good deed, but the worry is academics. Aren't your students losing valuable class time while baking cookies?"

"Not at all. They're learning valuable skills in a real-life situation. I realize my teaching style is not traditional but students learn by doing as well, maybe better, than by using only textbooks."

Biff took a pencil from his desk and tapped the end on a desk calendar. He was unusually fidgety today. Whoever complained must have clout. "Give me some specifics to share with the concerned parent."

"Who is it? Maybe if I spoke with him or her?"

"I don't want my teachers bothered with disgruntled parents. I will handle the situation."

"I appreciate that, Biff. You've always been great support." Which was all the more reason to be concerned this time. Why was he not standing behind her on the cookie project? Who was putting pressure on the principal? "The project utilizes math, economics, life skills, social ethics, research skills, art and science." She ticked them off on her fingers. "There are more. Is that enough?"

Biff scribbled on a notepad. "For now. You may have to articulate exactly how those work at some point, but we'll start here."

"I really don't want to lose this project, Biff. It's a high point for my students."

"As well as for their teacher who loves everything Christmas." With a half smile he bounced the pencil one final time. "Why don't we have dinner tonight and discuss this further?"

The offer caught Sophie as much by surprise as someone's objection to the cookie project. She sputtered a bit before saying, "Thank you, but I have to say no. I'm sorry."

Her thoughts went to Davey and the way he'd clung to her this morning. She couldn't wait to see him again and let him know she kept her promises. She'd phoned after lunch to say hello and see how he was doing. Kade had answered, assured her Davey was doing fine and was at that moment sound asleep on Ida June's couch. The memory of Kade's voice, clipped, cool and intriguing, lingered like a song she couldn't get out of her head.

No, she definitely did not want to have dinner with the principal.

"I've already made other plans."

Biff's face closed up again. He stuffed the pen in his shirt pocket. "Ah. Well, another time, then."

At the risk of encouraging him, Sophie nodded and quickly left his office. The mystery casserole churned in her stomach. As her boot heels tapped rhythmically on highly waxed white tile, she reviewed the unsettling conversation. As much as she wanted to believe Biff's dinner invitation was purely professional, she knew better. Carmen was right. The principal liked her. She liked him, too. It wasn't that. He was a good man, a by-the-book administrator who strove for excellence and expected the same from his staff. As a teacher, she appreciated him. But as a woman? She hadn't thought seriously about her boss, and given the buzz of interest she'd felt for Ida June's nephew, she never would.

Frankly, the concerns about her teaching methods weighed more heavily right now.

Would Biff go as far as vetoing the cookie project?

Chapter Three

Kade pushed back from the laptop perched on Ida June's worn kitchen table and rubbed the strain between his eyes. Hours of poking into every law-enforcement database he could access produced nothing about a missing mute boy named David. He'd chased a rabbit trail for the past hour only to discover the missing child had been found.

Hunching his shoulders high to relieve the tightness, he glanced past the narrow dividing bar into Ida June's living room. Davey still slept, curled beneath a red plaid throw on the 1970s sofa, a psychedelic monstrosity in red, green and yellow swirls that, ugly as sin, proved a napping boy's paradise. In sleep, Davey had released his beloved book to fall in the narrow space between his skinny body and the fat couch cushion. Sheba lay next to him, her golden head snuggled beneath his lax arm. She opened one eye, gave Kade a lazy look and went back to sleep.

"Traitor," he said, softly teasing. The boy had taken one look at the affable dog and melted. Sheba could never resist a kid. When Davey went to his knees in joyful greeting and threw his arms around her neck, Sheba claimed him as her own. He'd shared his lunch with her, a sight that had twisted in Kade's chest. The kid had been hungry, maybe for days, but he'd shared a ham sandwich with the well-fed dog. Whatever had happened to Davey hadn't broken him. It may very well have silenced him, but his soul was still intact.

Kade rubbed a frustrated hand over his whiskered jaw and asked himself for the dozenth time why he'd gotten involved. He knew the answer. He just didn't like it.

Leaving the pair, he poured himself another cup of coffee and went to finish the laundry. At the moment, Davey wore one of Kade's oversize T-shirts and a ridiculously huge pair of sweats tied double at the waist. Now, when he awoke, Davey's clothes would be as clean as he was.

Once the boy had been fed, cleaned and his clothes in the washer, Ida June had barked a few orders and gone to work at the little town square. With Kade's less-than-professional assistance, she'd been erecting a stable for the town's Christmas celebration. She'd promised to have it finished this week, and leaving Kade to "mind the store" and "find that boy's mama," Ida June had marched out he door with a final parting shot: "Promises are ike babies squalling in a theater—they should be carried out at once."

He was still smirking over that one. His mother's aunt was a colorful character, a spunky old woman who'd outlived two husbands, built her own business and half of her own house, drove like a maniac and spouted quotes like Bartlett. And if anyone needed a helping hand, she was there, though heaven help the man or woman who said she had a soft heart.

Kade removed Davey's pitiful jeans and sweatshirt from the dryer and folded them next to clean socks and underwear before tossing the washed sneakers into the still-warm drier. He set them on tumble with one of Ida June's fragrant ocean-breeze dryer sheets and left them to thump and bang.

He wasn't much on shopping any more than he was on doing laundry, especially at Christmas when the holly, jolly Muzak and fake everything abounded, but a single man learned to take care of business. The boy needed clothes, and unless Sophie Bartholomew or Ida June offered, he'd volunteer.

Sophie. The wholesome-looking teacher had played around the edges of his thoughts all day, poking in a little too often. Nobody could be that sweet and smiley all the time.

"Probably on crack," he groused, and then snorted at the cynical remark. A woman like Sophie probably wouldn't know crack cocaine if it was in her sugar bowl.

His cell phone jangled and he yanked the device from his pocket to punch Talk. With calls into various law-enforcement agencies all over the region, he hoped to hear something. Even though he was a stranger here, with few contacts and no clout, his federal clearances gave him access to just about anything he wanted to poke his nose into.

It had been a while since he'd wanted to poke into anything. When he turned over rocks, he usually found snakes.

He squeezed his eyes shut. The year undercover had skewed his perspective. He wasn't looking for snakes this time. He was looking for a boy's family.

One hand to the back of his neck, the other on the phone, he went to the kitchen window and stared blindly out at the gray sky as the voice on the other end gave him the expected news. Nothing.

He figured as much. A dumped kid might be big news in Redemption but to the rest of the world, Davey was another insignificant statistic.

Acid burned his gut—an ulcer, he suspected, though he'd avoided mentioning the hot pain to the shrink. Being forced by his superiors to talk to a head doctor was bad enough. No one was going to shove a scope down his throat and tell him to take pills and live on yogurt. He didn't do pills. Or yogurt. He'd learned the hard way that one pill, one drug, one time could be the end of a man.

He scrubbed his hands over his eyes. He was so tired. He couldn't help envying Davey and Sheba their sound sleep. He ached to sleep, to fall into that wonderful black land of nothingness for more than a restless hour at a time. The coffee kept him moving, but no amount of caffeine replaced a solid sleep. He took a sip, grimaced at the day-old brew and the growing gut burn. Yeah, yeah. Coffee made an ulcer worse. Big deal. It wasn't coffee that was killing him.

In the scrubbed-clean driveway outside the window, a deep purple Ford Focus pulled to a stop. The vehicle, a late-model job, was dirt-splattered from the recent rain, and the whitewalls needed a scrub. Why did women ignore the importance of great-looking wheels? The schoolteacher, brown hair blowing lightly in the breeze, hopped out, opened the back car door and wrestled out a bulging trash bag. Curious, Kade set aside his mug and jogged out to help.

"What's this?" he asked.

The afternoon sun, weak as a twenty-watt bulb, filtered through the low umbrella of stratus clouds and found the teacher's warm smile. There was something about her, a radiance that pierced the bleak day with light. Kade's troubled belly tingled.

She attracted him, plain and simple—a surprise given how dead he felt most of the time.

Her smile widening, Sophie shoved the black trash sack into his arms. She had a pretty mouth full lips with gentle creases along the edges like sideways smiles. "Davey needs clothes."

"You went shopping?" She'd barely had time to get here from school. And why the hefty bag?

"No." Her laugh danced on the chilly breeze and hit him right in the ulcer. "I know kids, lots of kids all sizes and shapes, who outgrow clothes faster than their parents can buy them. I made a few phone calls and voilà!" She hunched her shoulders, fingers of one hand spreading in the space between them like a starburst. "Davey is all fixed up." Perky as a puppy, she hoisted another bag. "This has a few toys in it. We were guessing size, so I hope something fits. The rest can go to the shelter."

"Bound to fit better than what he's wearing now." She was going to get a kick out of his impromptu outfit.

"How is he?" she asked as they carried the bags inside.

"Exhausted." Kade dumped his bag in a chair inside the living room and hitched his chin toward the ugly couch. "He's slept like a rock most of the day."

"What did the doctor say? Have we heard any news on where he came from? Where's Ida June?"

Shooting questions like an arcade blaster, Sophie moved past him into the room. A subtle wake of clean perfume trailed behind to tantalize his senses. Sunshine and flowers and—he sniffed once—coconut. She smelled as fresh and wholesome as she looked.

Amused by her chatter, he slouched at the bar and waited for her to wind down. "You finished?"

"For now." She stood over Davey and Sheba, a soft smile tilting her naturally curved lips. "Is this your dog?"

"Was until this morning."

She gave him that happy look again. She was lucky. No one had wiped away her joy. Life must have always been good in Sophie's world.

"A boy and a dog is a powerful combination," she said.

"Sheba's a sucker for kids."

"So is her master."

"Me?" Where did she get such a weird idea? He did his job. Did what he had to. And a dose of retribution was only just.

"So tell me, what did the doctor say?"

"Dehydrated and run-down but otherwise healthy. Nothing rest and nutrition won't fix." He'd been careful to ask the right questions and the child showed no signs of physical abuse. No outward signs.

"What about his voice?"

Kade nodded behind him to the kitchen. "Let's talk in here."

"Sure." Smart Sophie got the message. He didn't want to talk near the boy, not with the suspicions tearing at the back of his brain. With a lingering glance at Davey, she followed Kade to the kitchen.

"Want some coffee?" he asked.

"It's cold out." She rubbed her palms together. "A hot cup sounds great if it's already made."

"Coffee's always made."

She raised a dark, tidy eyebrow. "Chain drinker?"

"Safer than chugging Red Bull."

The answer revealed more than he'd intended. He went to the counter, more aware of her than he wanted to be and wondering, even though he didn't want to, what it would be like to be normal again the way she was. Normal and easy in her skin. Maybe that's what made her so pretty. She wasn't movie-star beautiful, although she warmed the room like an unexpected ray of sun across a shadow. Dark, soft, curving hair. Soft gray eyes. Clear, soft skin. Everything about Sophie Bartholomew was soft.

"What did the doctor say about Davey's voice?"

"He found no physical reason for Davey not to speak, though he did recommend a specialist." Kade poured two cups and held up the sugar bowl. Sophie shook her head. Figured. She was sweet enough. Kade loaded his with three spoons and stirred them in. "We'll have to leave that to social services."

Sophie grimaced. He got that. Social services did what they could, but who really *cared* about one little boy?

"Then there must be something mental or emo-ional, and he doesn't appear mentally handi-capped." She accepted the offered cup, sipped with her eyes closed. Kade, a detail man courtesy of his career, tried not to notice the thick curl of mink ashes against pearl skin. "Mmm. Perfect. Thanks."

"Which leaves us with one ugly conclusion." He took a hot gulp and felt the burn before the liquid ever hit his belly. The more he thought about what could have happened to Davey, the more his gut hurt. "Trauma."

"I wondered about that, but was hoping…" Her voice trailed off. She picked at the handle of her cup.

"Yeah, me, too."

Sophie's fingers went to her lips, flat now with concern for the little boy. She painted her finger-nails. Bright Christmas red with tiny silver snow-flakes. How did a woman do that?

"You think something happened that upset him so much he stopped talking?"

Jaw tight, Kade nodded. "So does the doc."

And if it took him the rest of his life, somebody somewhere was gonna pay.

Sophie studied the trim, fit man leaning against da June's mustard-colored wall. In long-sleeved

Henley shirt and blue jeans, dark brown hair
combed messily to one side, he could be any ordinary man, but she suspected he wasn't. Kade
McKendrick was cool to the point of chill with a
hard glint to wary eyes that missed nothing. He was
tough. Defensive. Dangerous.

Yet, he'd responded to Davey's need with concern, and he had a wry wit beneath the cynical twist
of that tight mouth. He didn't smile much but he
knew how. Or he once had. Her woman's intuition
said he'd been through some trauma himself. Her
woman's heart wanted to bake him cookies and fix
him.

A little troubled at the direction of her thoughts,
she raised her coffee mug, a shield to hide behind.
She didn't even know this guy.

"What could be so terrible that a child would stop
speaking?" she asked. "I can't imagine."

Something flickered in the stolid expression, a
twitch of muscle, the narrowing of coffee-colored
eyes in a hard face.

"I plan to find out."

"I heard you were a cop."

"Listening to gossip?"

She smiled. "Not all of it."

The admission caught him by surprise. He lightened, just a little, but enough for her to see his
humor. She didn't know why that pleased her, but
it did. Kade needed to lighten up and smile a little.

"I am." He went to the sink and dumped the remaining coffee, rinsed the cup and left it in the sink. "A cop, that is. Special units."

"You don't want to hear about the other rumors?"

He made a huffing noise. "Maybe later. You don't want to hear about the special units?"

"Maybe later." She smiled again, hoping he'd smile, too. He didn't. "The important thing is Davey. Your police experience should help us find his family."

"Us?"

"Well…" She wasn't a person to start something and not follow through. She'd been there when Davey was found and she didn't intend to walk away and leave him with all these unanswered questions. "I know the community really well. People trust me. They'll talk to me. I don't know the first thing about investigating a missing boy." She stopped, frowned. Davey wasn't missing exactly. "Or rather, a found boy, but I know how to deal with people."

Kade raised a palm. "Let's not get ahead of ourselves. It's early yet. Someone may come home from work tonight, find their son gone and call in. Problem solved."

"Do you think they will?" she asked hopefully.

"To be honest?" He dropped his arms to his sides, shot a look toward the living room. "No."

Something in the sudden clip of his voice chilled Sophie's bones. She frowned and leaned forward, propping her arms on the metal dinette. Ida June must have had this thing since the 1950s. "Have you worked in Missing Children before?"

She was almost certain he flinched, but if he did, he covered the emotion quickly.

"In a manner of speaking."

Sophie waited for an explanation, but when none was forthcoming, she asked, "Do you have any ideas? Any thoughts about where he came from or what happened?"

"A few." He crossed his arms again. She recognized the subconscious barrier he raised between them. What had happened to this man to make him so aloof? For a people person, he was a challenge. For a Christian, he was someone to pray for. For a single woman, he was dangerously attractive. What woman wouldn't want to delve behind those dark, mysterious eyes and into that cool heart to fix whatever ailed him?

"Care to share?" she asked.

He cocked his head, listening. "Davey's awake."

Sophie hadn't heard a sound, but she pushed away from the table and hurried past Kade to the sofa and the little boy who'd had her prayers all day. Behind her, a more troubling and troubled presence followed. She was in the company of two mysterious males and they both intrigued her.

"Hi, Davey." She sat on the edge of the couch, the warmth of Davey's sleep-drenched body pleas-

ant against her leg. Kade's big dog, a golden retriever, slid off the sofa and padded to her master.
He dropped a hand to her wide skull and stood like
a dark slab of granite watching as Davey looked
around in that puzzled "Where am I?" manner of
someone waking in a strange place.

"Remember me? I'm Sophie. My students call me
Miss B."

The towheaded child blinked stubby lashes and
rubbed the sleep from his eyes. He sat up, the blanket falling to his waist.

Sophie grinned up at Kade. "Your shirt?"

A wry twist to one side of his mouth, Kade nodded.
"My sweats, too. His clothes are in the dryer."

Davey pushed the cover away and stood. The
oversize black pants puddled around his feet. Sophie
laughed. "I need a camera."

Davey looked down, and then, too serious,
glanced from Sophie to Kade and back again, eyes
wide and uncertain.

"Guess what? We have some great new clothes
for you. You want to look through the bag and find
something you like?" She dragged the bag from the
chair with a plastic thud against green shag carpet
and pulled open the yellow tie. "There's a very cool
sweatshirt in here. And wait till you see this awe-
some jacket with a hood and secret zip-up pockets."

She was rewarded when Davey realized her mission and went to his knees next to the bag. Sophie held up a T-shirt. "What do you think?"

He nodded eagerly, then plunged his hands into the sack and removed a pair of cowboy boots. His whole body reacted. He hopped up, stumbled on his long pants and would have gone down if Kade, swift as a cat, hadn't caught him. "Easy, pard."

"I think he likes his new duds."

Davey held the boots up for Kade's inspection. Sophie watched with interest as the man pretended to consider before nodding his head. "Shoulda been a cowboy myself."

Davey's face broke into a wide smile. He plopped onto the floor and shoved at the too-long pants to find his feet. Sophie's smile widened. "Here, Davey. I think you could use some help."

Kade moved into action. "Why don't we find some jeans first and then try the boots?"

But Davey was already shoving his small feet into the brown-and-white-stitched footwear. His foot went in with an easy *whoosh* of skin against leather. Thrilled, smile wide enough to crack his cheeks, he leaned in to hug her from the side. Sophie's heart pinched. The boots were obviously too big, but Davey behaved as though she'd given him the best Christmas present of his life.

He levered himself up with her shoulder and attempted to clomp around, still grinning. The sweats puddled on the floor and tripped him up again.

Kade reached out to steady him, expression inscrutable. "Grab him some jeans. I'll help him change."

Sophie did as he asked, touched when Kade hoisted Davey under one arm and carted him, boots, jeans and all, sweats flopping in the empty space beneath Davey's feet, to another room. Sheba padded softly behind, her nose inches from Kade.

Minutes later Sophie heard a *clomp, clomp* as the trio returned, Davey dressed in clean jeans, a Dallas Cowboys sweatshirt and the too-big boots. Kade had dampened the child's pale hair and brushed away the bedhead.

"Well, don't you look handsome?"

Davey beamed and clomped to her. Sheba followed, her nose poked beneath his hand as though expecting him to fall at any moment and prepared to catch him.

"I think the clothes are a hit," Kade said.

"The boots are for certain." Sophie dipped in the bag. "Davey, we might as well go through these and see what else you like. You can keep anything that fits."

As they rummaged through the hand-me-downs, Sophie was a little too aware of Kade kneeling beside her, his taut arm brushing hers as they pulled clothes from the sack. There was a stealthy danger about him, a rigid control she assumed came from his work in law enforcement. Special units, he'd said. Now she wondered what he'd meant.

She was holding a blue dress shirt under Davey's chin, his little arms spread wide to test the sleeve length, when they heard a car in the drive.

"Ida June?" she asked.

A minute later, the doorbell chimed. "Apparently not."

Kade shoved to his feet and went to answer. Sophie heard voices but thought nothing of them until Kade returned, trailed by a man in a business suit. Sophie's pleasure seeped away.

"Hello, Howard." She knew the social worker from school and the times he'd come to interview teachers about a child's well-being. Good at his job, professional and thorough, she'd always been glad to have him in a child's corner. Until today.

"Sophie, how are you?"

"Great." She'd been better. "Is everything okay? Davey's doing fine here, as you can see. We're sorting through some clothes my students donated."

"Nice of you to take an interest. Tell your students thanks. We appreciate all you've done. Both of you."

"No problem. Davey's a good boy."

"The Cunninghams will be glad to hear that."

Dread pulled at Sophie's belly. "The Cunninghams?"

"The foster family. We got lucky. They can take him today."

Sophie made a small sound of distress. "He's

doing fine here, Howard. Why not leave him with Kade and Ida June?"

"Neither has foster-parenting credentials or clearances. The Cunninghams are paper-ready."

"You've known Ida June forever and Kade is in law enforcement."

"The system doesn't work that way. Sorry. The Cunninghams are a good family with experience with special-needs children. He'll do well with them." Howard hitched the crease of his navy slacks and went to one knee in front of Davey. "My name is Mr. Prichard, Davey. You'll be coming with me today. There's a family waiting to meet you. You're going to like it at their house."

Davey frowned, bewildered gaze moving from Howard to Sophie and Kade.

"Howard," Sophie said, beseeching.

"I have a job to do, Sophie. Our department comes under enough fire as it is. We have to follow procedures." The social worker rose, matter-of-fact. "If you'd gather his belongings, he can take them along."

"This is all he has." The plastic bag crinkled as she pushed at it. A few hand-me-down clothes and an oversize pair of boots.

"More than most have, sad to say. Come along, Davey." The man grasped Davey's hand and started for the door. Davey jerked away and ran to Kade, throwing his arms around the familiar man's legs.

Sheba whined and pushed against Davey's back. He fell against her neck and clung.

"Let him stay." Kade's voice was hard as granite.

Howard ignored the request. "Come now, Davey." When the boy didn't obey, the social worker scooped Davey into his arms and headed to the car. Davey squirmed but didn't make a sound. The silence was more terrible than any amount of crying.

Sophie followed, fighting tears, her throat clogged with emotion. She pushed Davey's beloved book into his hands. "It's okay, Davey. I know the Cunningham family. They're nice people. I'll call you. I'll come over and see you. We'll find your family. I promise. I promise. Don't be afraid."

Tense fingers caught her arm. Kade, face as hard as ice, said, "Don't make promises."

Sophie stopped in the driveway next to the black Taurus and forced an encouraging smile as the social worker buckled the little lost boy into the backseat. Beside her, Kade said nothing, but anger seethed from him, hot against the evening chill. She lifted her hand, waved and held on to the fake smile while the car backed into the street and pulled away.

A cold wind swirled around her, lifted her hair, scattered scratchy brown leaves across the pavement. The dark sedan turned the corner, out of sight now.

Sophie lowered her hand and stood dejected in the bleak afternoon. What a sad way to spend Christmas.

Be with him, Jesus.

Even though her prayer was heartfelt, Sophie knew little comfort. The sight of Davey's tormented face pressed against the window glass with silent tears streaming would stay with her forever.

Chapter Four

Kade wanted to punch something. Fists tight against his sides, he glared at the departing car, shocked by his reaction. He wasn't supposed to get personally involved. But he *was* supposed to protect and serve. With Davey gone to strangers, how could he do that?

Sophie touched him. A gentle hand to his outer elbow. A comforting squeeze and release. His muscles tensed. He turned from staring down Hope Avenue, a useless occupation considering the car was long gone, to meet the teacher's gaze. He didn't say what he was thinking. A woman like her wouldn't want to know, and as the dismayed shrink had discovered, Kade was not one to vomit his emotions all over someone else anyway.

"I don't know what to do," she said.

"Nothing we can do."

"This doesn't feel right. I don't know why exactly.

We barely know Davey, but I'm worried about him. He seemed comfortable with us."

"Yeah." Kade pivoted toward the house. "Might as well get out of the wind. Want to come in?"

"No, I should go. I—" She pushed aside a blowing curve of hair, only to let it blow right back across her face.

"Come in. Finish your coffee." He wasn't ready for her to leave. They shared a common concern and a common ache. Sophie was a nice woman, the kind a man didn't blow off and leave standing in his driveway.

She didn't argue but fell in step beside him. Her height was average, as was his, but his stride was longer. She picked up her pace. "I hadn't read the book. I promised to read his book."

He'd told her not to make promises. Promises got broken. He pushed open Ida June's front door, a bright red enameled rectangle festooned with a smelly cedar wreath the size of an inner tube. "He'll be okay."

"The Cunninghams are good people. They live on a farm."

Sheba met them at the door, body language asking about Davey.

Sophie stroked the golden ears. "She didn't want him to leave, either."

"No."

"I'll call Cybil Cunningham tonight and check on him. She won't mind."

"Good." He went to the kitchen, stuck their coffee mugs in the microwave to heat. "This doesn't end here."

The words came out unexpectedly but he meant them. The microwave beeped and he popped the door open to hand Sophie her heated coffee.

She took the mug with both hands and sipped, gray gaze watching him above the rim. "You're going to search for his family?"

"I'm searching for answers. It's what I do. And I'll find them." The stir in his blood was far more potent than the acid in his belly. Finding answers for Davey gave him focus, a mission, something to do besides relive failure.

"The police will do that, won't they?" She set the mug on the metal table and drew out a chair.

Kade shrugged. A lot she knew about law enforcement. "They'll try. For a while. But if the trail grows cold, Davey will go on the back burner."

"And be stuck in the social system."

"Right." Restless, he didn't join her at the table, but he liked seeing her there, calm to his anxious. How did she do that? How did she shift into serene gear after what had just happened? He knew she'd been emotional when Davey left. He'd watched her struggle, saw her pull a smile out of her aching heart for Davey's sake. Now she drew on some inner reserve as though she trusted everything would work out for the best. "I talked to Jesse Rainmaker an hour ago. Nothing. Nothing on the databases, either."

"I don't understand that. If your child was missing, wouldn't you call the police?"

She was as naive as a baby, a cookie-baking optimist. The thought tickled the corners of his eyes. "Maybe, maybe not."

Her cup clinked against the metal top. "I don't know much about this kind of thing, Kade, but I want to do something to help Davey find his family. Please tell me what you're thinking."

He was positive she didn't want to hear it all. "I can think of a couple of scenarios. One, his family doesn't know he's missing."

"That's unlikely, isn't it?"

"Sometimes parents are out of the house, at work, partying. They come home a day or two later and find their kid gone. By tomorrow, someone should raise a shout if they're going to."

"What else?"

"His parents don't want him." He saw by her reaction how hard that was for her to comprehend. "It happens, Sophie."

"I know. Still…" Some of the Christmas cheer leached from her eyes.

"Davey is mute. A family might not be able to deal with that. Or worse, his parents may not be in the picture. Or he could have been missing for so long they aren't actively looking anymore."

A frown wrinkled the smooth place between her fascinating eyebrows. A face like hers shouldn't have to frown.

"Are you saying he might be a kidnap victim?"

"He's a little young to be a runaway. I searched the database of the Center for Missing and Exploited Children and came up with nothing, but that doesn't mean he's not a victim. It only means no one has reported him missing."

"Are you saying a parent would ignore the fact that their child is gone?"

"It happens. Kids are a commodity. You can buy them on the internet."

Sophie lifted a weak hand in surrender. "Don't."

Ignoring the problem didn't make it go away, but he bit back the obvious comment. Sophie was small-town sweet and innocent. She hadn't seen the dark side. She hadn't lived in the back alleys of the underworld.

Kade poured another cup of coffee, then shoved the mug aside to take milk from the fridge. Something cool and bland might soothe the lava burning his guts.

"Kade?"

He swallowed half a glass of milk before answering. "Yeah?"

"You want to order some fifth-grade cookies to go with that milk?"

In spite of himself, he laughed. She was a piece of work, this cookie lady. "You're going to hound me."

"Gently. Merrily. It's a Christmas project. So," she said, with quiet glee, "how many dozen?"

"What am I going to do with a bunch of cookies?"

"Eat them, give them as gifts, have a Christmas party. The possibilities are limitless."

"I don't do the Christmas thing."

She didn't go there and he was grateful. He wasn't up to explaining all the reasons he couldn't muster any Christmas spirit. Or any kind of spirit for that matter. His faith hadn't survived the dark corners of south Chicago.

"Everyone eats cookies." Her smile tilted the corners of a very nice, unenhanced mouth. He wondered if she had a guy.

"A dozen. Now leave me alone."

His gruff reply seemed to delight, rather than insult. "You old Scrooge. I'll get you for more."

Wouldn't that be a stupid sight? Him with a bunch of Santas and stars and Christmas trees to eat all by himself. Or better yet, he'd stand on the street corner back home and hand them out. See how long before he got arrested.

"We were talking about the boy," he said.

She shrugged, a minimal motion of shoulders and face. "Your stomach is bothering you. You needed a distraction."

Kade narrowed his eyes at her. "The cookie lady is a mind reader?"

"People watcher."

She *had* distracted him, although the cookie conversation was not as powerful as the woman herself. A less careful man could get lost in all that sugary sweetness.

He tilted his head toward the garage and the clatter of Ida June's old truck engine chugging to a halt. Before he could say "She's here," his inimitable aunt sailed through the back entrance and slammed the door with enough force to make Sheba give one startled yip.

"I heard what happened." Disapproval radiating from every pore, Ida June slapped a sunflower knitting bag the size of his gym bag onto the butcher-top counter. "I'll give Howard Prichard a piece of my mind and he'll know the reason why. Silliest thing I ever heard of. Jerk a terrified child from a perfectly fine place and take him to live with a bunch of strangers."

"We're strangers, too," Kade said mildly. Seeing her riled up cooled him down even though he appreciated her fire.

"Don't sass, nephew. What are you going to do about this?" With a harrumph, she folded her arms across the front of her overalls. Sheba, the peace-maker, nudged her knee.

Kade imitated her crossed arms and slouched against the refrigerator. "Find his family."

"I expected as much. Good to hear it." Ida June gave the dog an absent pat. Then as if she'd just realized someone else occupied the kitchen, she said, "Hello, Sophie. You selling cookies?"

Sophie set her cup to one side. "It's that time of year."

"Put me down for five dozen. Did you get this nephew of mine to buy any?"

The pretty mouth quivered. "A dozen."

Kade was tempted to roll his eyes because he knew what was to come from his incorrigible aunt.

"He'll have to do better than that. Stay after him."

"I plan to."

"I'm still in the room," he said mildly. The refrigerator kicked on, the motor vibrating against his tense back. "The least you can do is wait until I'm gone to gang up on me."

Aunt Ida June gave him a mock-sour look. "Crybaby. Is Sophie staying for supper? I made that lasagna last night and you didn't eat enough of it to feed a gnat. I refuse to feed it to Sheba." When the dog cocked her head, Ida June amended. "Maybe a bite. Well, is Sophie staying or not?"

Kade arched an inquiring eyebrow in Sophie's

direction. He didn't mind if she stayed for dinner. Might be interesting to know her better.

He waited for her answer. An insistent, perplexing hope nudged up inside him.

Sophie rose from the table and pushed in the chair, as polite and tidy as he would have expected. Kade liked what he saw, and not just the fact that she was pretty as sunshine and looked good in a sweater. He liked the feminine way her fingertips glided along the top of the chair rung before straightening the hem of her blouse. And the way she met Ida June's gaze with straight-on, clear and honest eye contact.

A student of human nature, Kade could spot pretense in a second. There was nothing false about Sophie Bartholomew.

He hoped she'd stay for dinner.

"Thank you, Miss Ida June," she said. "But I have to say no. I promised to drop by my dad's this evening and help put up his Christmas decorations."

Kade's ulcer mocked him. All right, so she had a life. Other than Davey, she had no reason to stick around here.

"You're a good daughter," Ida June said, smacking her lips together with satisfaction. "You'll make a fine wife."

"I have a great dad." If Sophie thought a thing about Ida June's blatant "wife" remark, she didn't let on. Apparently, the citizens of Redemption were accustomed to his aunt's habit of saying exactly what she thought.

Sophie took her coffee cup to the sink and turned on the warm water. Above the *whoosh,* she asked, "How's the stable coming along?"

"Leave that cup in the sink. Kade's gotta be useful for something around here." Ida June shouldered Kade to the side and yanked a casserole from the refrigerator. She banged the sturdy glass dish on the counter and dug in the cabinets for foil and a spatula. The woman slammed and banged in the kitchen the same way she did on a job. With purpose and sass.

"You'll take your dad some lasagna." From Sophie's quiet acceptance, Kade figured she knew not to argue with Ida June. "Stable's nearly done. Would have been if Kade had been there. Makes me so aggravated not to be able to carry a four-by-eight sheet of plywood by myself." She flexed an arm muscle and gave it a whap. "Puny thing."

"Nobody would accuse you of being puny, Ida June." Kade moved to Sophie's side and reached for the coffee mug.

She scooted but didn't turn loose of the cup. She did, however, flash him that sunny smile, only this one carried a hint of his aunt's sass. "I can do it."

"Yeah?" he arched a brow.

She arched one, too. "Yeah."

Was the cookie lady flirting with him?

They jockeyed for position for a few seconds while Kade examined the interesting simmer of energy buzzing around the pair of them like honeybees in a glass jar, both dangerous and sweet. Danger he understood, but sweet Sophie didn't know what she was bumping up against.

Ten minutes later, he walked her out the front door, leaving Ida June to heat a spicy casserole that would torture him again tonight.

He opened the car door for Sophie, stood with one hand on the handle as she slid gracefully onto the seat. At some point in the day she'd changed her clothes from a long blue sweater to a dark skirt and white blouse. She looked the part of a teacher. Weird that he'd notice. "Don't worry about the kid."

Keys rattled as she dug in the pocket of a black jacket. "I won't. But I *will* pray for him."

His teeth tightened. "You pray. I'll find answers."

A cloud passing overhead shadowed her usual cheer. "We can do both."

"Right." God listened to people like Sophie. Kade still believed that much.

She started the engine and yet he remained in the open car door, wanting to say something reassuring and not knowing how. Life, he knew, did not always turn out the way it should.

"Kade?" she said.

"Yeah?"

She reached out and placed her hand on his sleeve.

Her warmth, or maybe the thought of it, seeped through the thick cotton.

"Everything will be all right." Her gray eyes smiled, serious but teasing, too. "I promise."

The tables had turned. She was the one doing the reassuring. For two beats he even believed her.

Then he said, "Don't make promises," and shut the door.

"Dad, have you ever met Kade McKendrick?"

Sophie stood on a stepladder propped against her father's brick house, feeding tiny blue lightbulbs into equally tiny sockets. Next to her, on another stepladder, her dad attached strands of Christmas lights to the gabled eaves.

"Ida June's nephew? Yes, I've run into him a time or two. Why?"

"What was your impression?"

"Polite. Watchful. A man with something on his mind."

"Hmm." Yes, she saw those things. He was wounded, too, and maybe a little sour on the world. Beneath that unhealthy dose of cynicism, she also saw a man who didn't back down, who did what he promised. Although he had this thing about not making any promises at all. "Hmm."

Her father paused, one hand braced against brick to turn his head toward her. "What does that *hmm* of yours mean?"

"I don't know, Dad. Nothing really." She didn't know how to put into words the curious interest Kade had stirred up. "He says he'll find Davey's family."

"Maybe he will," her dad said. "I heard he was an agent for the DEA."

"He mentioned special units, whatever those are."

"Could be DEA or any of the other highly trained groups. Seems strange, don't you think, for him to be here in Redemption doing odd jobs with a great aunt?"

She took another bulb from her jacket pocket and snapped it into the tiny slot. "Maybe he's simply a nice guy helping out an older relative."

"Ida June? Older?" Dad snorted and turned back to his task. "I won't tell her you said that."

Sophie laughed. "Thanks."

"So what are you ruminating about?"

"When I mentioned praying for Davey, Kade threw up a wall of resistance. He did the same thing when I mentioned Christmas."

"Lots of non-Christians get uncomfortable with God talk, but Christmas is a different matter. Maybe something bad happened during the holidays?" He paused to take another strand of lights from her outstretched hand. "Or maybe the guy's a jerk."

"I don't think so, Dad. He was kind to Davey. Almost tender. You should have seen the pair of them digging through that bag of clothes."

"You like him, don't you?"

Her heart jumped, a reaction she didn't quite get. She *liked* everyone. "Beyond his kindness to Davey, I barely know him."

"I knew your mother was *the one* the minute I laid eyes on her."

Like a fly on her hamburger, the remark soured Sophie's stomach. How could Dad speak casually and without bitterness when Sophie still felt the disappointment as keenly as she had five years ago?

She pushed one final bulb into a socket and backed down the ladder. "Are we putting the sleigh on the roof this year?"

If Dad noticed the change in subjects, he didn't let on. With a sparkle in his eyes and the nip of wind reddening his cheeks, he asked, "Do elves make toys? Does Santa have a list of naughty and nice?"

Mark Bartholomew was almost as Christmas-crazy as his daughter, and every year they worked for days decorating first his house and then her little cottage. No matter how cold and fierce the wind or how many other activities they had going, this had become their tradition since the divorce. She'd started the practice so that the first holiday without Mom would be easier for him, but now she treasured this special time with her father.

"Did you see the new displays at Case's Hardware Store?"

"Saw them. Bought the praying Santa and the lighted angel." He clattered down the ladder.

Shivering once, Sophie slapped her upper arm for warmth. "The one with the flapping wings?"

"He's in the garage."

"Sweet." They exchanged high fives, the usual slap muffled by Sophie's gloves.

"I think we've done all the damage to the electric bill we can manage for one day," he said and started toward the porch.

Sophie followed her dad past the inflated snowman, through a door decked with green lighted garland and wreath, and into the living room where the old artificial tree their family had used for years now stood proudly in one corner. She knew he put the tree up for her sake, to keep the family tradition alive even with Mother gone. Life wasn't the same but it was still Christmas.

With a sigh, she settled into Dad's big leather recliner while he fiddled with the switch on the musical bells and set them chiming. Lights blinked frantically to the tune of "Carol of the Bells." Cleo the resident cat princess, mewed in plaintive protest and wound herself around Sophie's feet.

"Get up here, girl." Sophie patted her leg. The aging family pet blinked long blue eyes. Then to make sure Sophie remembered that *she* was the boss, Cleo ignored the offered lap and leaped easily to the back of the chair and stretched out.

"As independent as ever." Dad made one last adjustment to the lighted tree and stood. Colored light

lickered over his worn University of Oklahoma
sweatshirt and reflected a rosy glow on his skin.

"Queen of her domain." Sophie reached over one
shoulder to rub the arrogant cat. "The two of you
re quite a pair."

"True. She's my buddy."

Cleo batted Sophie's fingers with soft claws and
urred. The Siamese had been Mom's cat, but she'd
left her pet behind along with her family. Sophie
lought, not for the first time, how lonely Dad must
e in this once-noisy, active house with only Cleo
or company.

"Have you talked to Todd lately?" Her brother
nd his family were in the military, stationed in
t. Hood. Holidays presented a challenge for them,
specially with his wife's family in Florida.

"A couple of days ago. They're going to her folks'
his year."

"Imagine that," she teased. "Choosing the Sun-
hine State over cold and blustery Oklahoma."

"I like cold and blustery."

"Me, too. It feels like Christmas."

She had her father, her church, her students and
nost of all, her Lord. Christmas in Redemption,
lustery wind and all, would be blessed and beau-
ful. If she sometimes wished for a family of her
wn, especially at Christmas, it was only natural.
hirty, that suspicious benchmark of spinsterhood,
vas only a few years away. Not that age bothered

her all that much. It wasn't age that made her rest
less sometimes. But the occasional ache for a home
filled with love and laughter and a husband an
children was undeniably present. Christmas, espe
cially, was family time.

Her thoughts roamed to Davey and then to Kade
What kind of Christmas would they have? Kade
said he didn't "do the Christmas thing." What di
he mean? Was Dad right? Had some painful ever
turned him off to the greatest event in history?

Cellophane crinkled as Dad handed her a red
and-white candy cane. The memory of Davey's boo
flashed in her head. Hadn't there been a candy can
on the front? Cybil Cunningham was a good woma
with a heart for disabled children. Sophie hope
she'd read Davey's book to him. Maybe she'd driv
out to see him tomorrow if Kade or the police didn
find where he belonged. She prayed they would.

She gave the peppermint a lick, her first tast
of the new Christmas season. "Do I get your spe
cial secret-recipe Bartholomew hot cocoa to go wit
this?"

"I'm on my way to the kitchen." Sophie started t
rise, but her Dad waved her back down. "Sit. You'r
still not old enough to be trusted with the famil
secret."

With a happy hum, he disappeared around th
wall. Sophie heard the clatter of drawers open
ing and a pot rattle against the stove top. For thes

w moments, she let herself be Daddy's little girl
gain, knowing how much pleasure he took in feel-
g needed.

She kicked off her shoes and curled her chilled
et beneath her, listening to the tinny melody of
oy to the World" from the Christmas tree.

Her world *was* full of joy. She wished she could
ackage the feeling and share it with those who
und no pleasure in the season.

Kade encroached again, his handsome face seri-
us, the brown eyes dark with some secret angst.
ad something happened to steal his joy? Or was
just a guy with a negative attitude?

The cool, sweet peppermint melted on her tongue.
rom the kitchen arose the warm scent of milk and
ocolate. The tree sparkled, a candle dripped cin-
amon-scented wax, Cleo purred, warm and con-
nt against Sophie's neck.

Maybe Kade had never had this. Maybe he didn't
ow what he was missing.

Sophie took a deep pull on the sweet candy.

Maybe Kade was a Grinch by accident and
eded help to find his Christmas spirit.

She offered up a quick prayer, certain the
ord had something special in mind for Scrooge
cKendrick this year.

Why else would a big-city cop show up in a small,
hristmas-crazy town just in time for the holidays?

Chapter Five

The telephone rang at six. Kade grabbed the re
ceiver on the first ring.

"McKendrick," Kade snapped before remember
ing. This was his aunt's home, not his work phon
He scrubbed a hand over his hair.

"I apologize for waking you," the male voice sai

Waking him? Wouldn't that be nice? He'd l
Sheba out hours ago. Since then, he'd been lyin
on the ugly psychedelic sofa twiddling his thumb

"I'm up. Who's this?"

"Jesse Rainmaker at the police station."

The man worked long hours. "You have inform
tion on Davey?"

A hesitation. "We have a problem."

Kade's fingers tightened on the handset. "Wi
Davey? What kind of problem? Is he all right?"

"I was hoping you'd know. He ran away from t
Cunninghams sometime in the night. Mrs. Cu

ningham got up around three to look in on him and he was gone."

Kade fell back against the couch cushions and squinted at the shadowy ceiling. "You think he's a runner? He's done this before?"

The furnace kicked on, shuddering in its old age. Faint heat eked from the floor vent to his cool sock feet. It was cold outside. Had Davey worn his new, hand-me-down jacket? The one with the blue race car on the back?

"Maybe. But a boy like that, without a voice, he's in danger wandering around alone." Rainmaker sighed, weariness heavy across the line. "The social worker told me how he reacted at your place. I thought you'd want to know."

Oh, yeah, Davey was in danger, all right. He couldn't ask for help. He couldn't even yell. And Kade definitely wanted to know. Sometime in the long hours of sleeplessness, the defenseless, tow-headed boy with the worried face had become personal.

"Did you notify Sophie?" The woman had plagued him all night, too, with her Suzy Snowflake personality and soft gray eyes. Davey had latched on to her, and she'd be upset about this turn of events. He wished he could spare her the worry. Nothing she could do about it, but she'd want to know.

"I'll leave that to you," Rainmaker said. "My deputies are searching around the Cunningham home. We could use some help, someone Davey likes."

"Give me directions." Kade scrambled for a pen and paper, not trusting his memory in strange territory—another hard lesson learned.

Jesse rattled off a series of section lines and local landmarks, then rang off with a "Thanks." Kade needed no thanks. He needed to find that boy.

Already dressed except for boots and coat, he shrugged into those, debating the phone call to Sophie. He wouldn't mind hearing her voice but not this way, not as the bearer of bad news.

Gritting his teeth, he whipped out his cell phone and punched in her name, glad they'd exchanged numbers, though at the time, he hadn't been thinking about Davey. He'd been thinking about those soft gray eyes and a softer smile.

Wishing for a pot of coffee, he listened in growing dismay at the *brrr* in his ear. This was Saturday. She would sleep late. Her voice mail clicked on.

"Merry Christmas," the recording said in that candy-coated voice. "You've reached Sophie Bartholomew. Please leave a message."

Easier this way, he thought. Much easier. At least for him.

Acid pooled in his belly. He rubbed the spot.

"Sophie, Kade McKendrick. Give me a call when you get this."

Why couldn't he do things the easy way? Why hadn't he just told her the situation and moved on?

He knew why. According to the shrink he had some kind of superhero complex. He could carry the weight. He could save the world.

Right. He snorted derisively. Tell that in the back alleys of Chicago.

When the phone in his hand suddenly rang, he almost dropped it. A quick glance told him Sophie had gotten the message.

"Hey," he said. "Sorry I woke you."

"You didn't. I was in the shower."

He carefully avoided going there. He was, after all, a man. "The police chief called."

"Davey?" Concern laced the word. Kade hated hearing it, hated knowing he'd put the worry there.

"He's run away from the Cunninghams."

She sucked in a gasp. "Oh, no."

"I'm headed out there now to help with the search. Thought you'd want to know."

"I'm coming. I'll meet you there."

"Get ready. I'll pick you up." He hadn't meant to offer, but he liked the idea of Sophie's soothing presence in his car. "You know the way?"

"Yes."

"Good. I don't."

He'd started to hang up when Sophie said quietly, "It's really cold this morning."

He understood her meaning. Davey was out there.

"Yeah." The chill in Ida June's house had kicked on the wheezing furnace numerous times during the night. "We'll find him, Sophie. Don't worry."

"Promise?" Her teasing words warmed him. He could hear her moving around, getting ready as they talked. He should hang up, but he was reluctant to let her go.

"No promises. Just action."

"I like the sound of that. Action and prayer work every time, and I'm already praying. God knows where Davey is."

"You let me know if He tells you."

He expected her to go all defensive on him, but instead she laughed. "I will. Have you had breakfast yet?"

Weird question. "No."

"I have coffee ready in the pot and yogurt in the fridge."

He made a face at the yogurt. "Bring me coffee and I'm your slave forever."

That warm, throaty chuckle filled his head. "I'm going to remember that."

They had a runaway kid to find and he was flirting with a schoolteacher. No wonder he'd lost his edge. Try as he might, he couldn't resist. And he didn't try too hard.

"Kade?"

"Yeah?"

"I'm joking around to keep from being afraid."

Her admission softened him. If he wasn't careful he'd never get his edge back. "It's cold and dark and the Cunninghams live several miles out in the country." He heard her swallow. "Davey has to be scared."

"We'll find him."

Phone against his ear, he made his way through the kitchen toward the garage. He flipped the exterior light switch and started down the two steps toward his car.

"Well." He stopped dead still.

"What is it?"

"I don't think we're going to find him."

A pause hummed anxiously over the distance. "Why?"

Curled in the corner on Sheba's fluffy bed, with the big dog wrapped around him protectively, Davey lay fast asleep, his book clasped to his skinny chest. He wore the zippered jacket Sophie had given him.

"He found us first."

Sophie didn't consider anything odd about rushing over to Ida June's house at six in the morning. She pulled into the short concrete drive before the streetlights went out and the first streaks of sun broke the horizon.

Looking lethally male beneath the golden glow of porch light, Kade let her in. A kick of attraction hit Sophie in the empty stomach. Now that she knew

Davey was safely in Kade's care, she took the time to explore the feeling. She hadn't been attracted this way in a long time, and considering Kade's dark broodiness, she was a little concerned by her judgment.

He hadn't shaved yet, naturally, given the time of morning, and a scruffy shadow of whiskers outlined his jaw and mouth. The bottom lip was fuller than the top and held in a grim line, as tightly controlled as his emotions. Everything about Kade McKendrick was close to the vest. His hair stuck up here and there, too, a messy look she found deliciously appealing. He looked like the kind of man with a holster under his shirt and a gun in the back of his jeans, the kind of man who'd fight for those he loved.

Be careful, Sophie.

She thrust a carton of yogurt at him. "Breakfast."

Kade lifted an eyebrow but didn't accept her offer. "You said coffee."

His male grumpiness tickled her. She sniffed the air, certain she whiffed fresh coffee already brewing. "Not a morning person?"

Eyes, dark as her favorite chocolate and more secret than the CIA, mocked her.

"*You* obviously are," he said.

"I am." She couldn't help waking up full of energy and happiness. Life was good. Mornings brought a clean slate, an empty new twenty-four hours to enjoy. "I'm also a woman of my word. Try this while yours is brewing." She handed over the thermos. "If it's any consolation, my dad hates yogurt, too."

"Man thing. You could have brought cookies instead." His tone was somewhere between a grouse because she hadn't and a tease. She liked when Kade teased. It was as if having fun was buried somewhere inside and on occasion bubbled to the surface like lava too long compressed. She'd have to work on unearthing his happy side more often.

"We can make cookies later," she said, and suddenly the idea of bumping around in a spice-scented kitchen with Kade sounded like a great way to spend a Saturday.

"Davey might like that."

She wanted to ask if Kade liked the idea, too, but she figured now was a good time to get her runaway brain under control.

"Is he still asleep?" They were standing in the entry, her view into the living area blocked by Kade's lithe, jean-clad body.

Kade nudged his chin to one side. "Back there. He needed a real bed for a change."

The reminder that Davey had likely slept out in the open for some time took her mind off the deadly handsome lawman. "May I look in on him?"

He set the thermos on the table—a sacrifice she knew—and led the way down a short hall to a bedroom. The door was open and Davey lay on his back covered to the chin. A furry dog snout was propped on his chest.

"Sheba won't let him out of her sight," Kade said in an undertone.

Sophie nodded. "As if she knows he needs her."

"She knows."

They watched the sleeping boy and dog for another minute. Sophie grew more aware of the room, of the masculine trappings. A jacket here, a pair of boots there, the faint, lingering scent of male grooming. In one corner leaned a battered guitar. This was Kade's bedroom, although the covers on the bed were ruffled only where Davey slept. Had Kade not been to bed last night?

Davey squirmed in his sleep, and a frown passed over the small face. Sheba nuzzled his cheek, and Davey, eyes still closed, wrapped both arms around the dog's neck and settled.

Kade tugged Sophie's elbow. Even though she wanted to stay and watch the sweetness that was dog and Davey at rest, she trailed Kade back down the short hall to Ida June's blue-and-yellow kitchen. Colors of the sun and the sky, she thought, as though Kade's aunt wanted the beauty and freshness of a June day year-round. Sophie got that, although Christmas colors were her favorite.

"Have you notified the sheriff and the Cunninghams that Davey is here?" she asked, and then anwered just as quickly. "Of course you have. Dumb question. You were a cop."

"Am." Kade poured himself a cup of coffee from her thermos.

"Pardon?"

"I *am* a cop. On R & R for a few months."

"You'll go back, then?"

"To work? Sure. Chicago?" He took a sip of coffee, closed his eyes either to savor the taste or to brace himself for the jolt. "The jury's still out."

She took the thermos from him and poured her own cup. "As in a real jury or metaphorically speaking?"

Kade smirked. "Both, actually. You want cream or sugar with that?"

"Yogurt."

His hand, halfway to his lips with another shot of caffeine, froze. "In your coffee? That's sick."

"I know." She gleefully stirred in a spoon, mostly to watch his reaction. Finally, he'd let his face show his true feelings.

He watched in horrified fascination as if she was about to eat a live snake. "You didn't do that yesterday."

"You didn't have yogurt." She took a satisfied sip.

Kade made a gagging noise.

Sophie giggled, almost spewing the mouthful. "Stop."

His nostrils flared with humor. "You're doing that to mess with my head."

She didn't remember when she'd started spooning yogurt into coffee, probably in college on a silly dare. Discovering she liked the odd, grainy combination had been the real surprise, although she normally reserved her yogurt coffee for quiet, alone times. Others didn't react well, as Kade so perfectly and delightfully demonstrated.

"Mostly. Is Ida June already up and out or are we disturbing her sleep?"

"We won't disturb her. Saturday is sleep day. She pokes earplugs in her ears, slides one of those weird masks over her eyes and threatens to disembowel anyone who opens her bedroom door before noon."

Sophie shook her head, amused. Ida June Click was, as her father said, a pistol. "Have you two always been close?"

"No." The teasing light flickered out. Oddly abruptly, he pushed out of the chair, went to the sink where he braced his hands to look out the window. Sophie had a feeling he didn't really see Ida June's backyard. And she wondered what can of worms she'd inadvertently opened inside the terse cop. Whatever had brought Kade to his great-aunt' home and to Redemption had followed him here un resolved.

Unsure where to tread, Sophie quietly sipped he coffee and waited him out. She studied him, lean waist and wedge-shaped torso taut, the leashed strength in his bent arms quivering with some deep emotion.

"I'm going to fight them over Davey," he said softly.

Puzzling, interesting man. "I am, too."

He whirled then as if he'd expected argument and gave one short nod. "Good. We're on the same page. He's not going back. One of us will take him."

"Until his family is found."

The heavy dose of doubt shadowed his secret eyes again. "Nearly eighty percent of runaways and throwaways are never reported missing by their families. Did you know that?" He tossed the numbers out as in challenge, teeth tight, eyes narrowed. "Eighty percent."

Throwaways? Never reported? Did such horrors really happen? "I can't believe Davey is either. He's young and cute and this is Oklahoma!"

She saw the eye roll he held in check and practically heard his thoughts. She was naive, a Pollyanna, sheltered.

"He's also handicapped. Granted, Davey's a little younger than usual, but facts are facts. Sometimes no one cares if a kid disappears."

Sophie didn't want to believe him. Children were a treasure from the Lord, not discardable afterthoughts. But Kade's adamant anger gave her a peek inside his head. He spoke from experience and that experience had left him bleeding.

Lord, You've put this man and this child in my life for a purpose. What now?

A quiet rustle of movement stopped the conversation as Davey rounded the corner into the kitchen. With sleepy eyes and a bedhead of pale, unruly hair, he was the cutest thing. Heart melting like a hot marshmallow, Sophie hoped he hadn't heard the unsettling conversation. She cut a glance toward Kade and marveled at the instant change in him. He'd gone from Doberman-like fierceness to the gentleness of the golden dog trailing the child into the kitchen.

"Hey, buddy." He went down on one knee in front of the little boy. "Feel better?"

Davey nodded, then walked into Kade's chest and snuggled his chin into his hero's shirt. Kade's eyelids fell closed. One blunt-nailed hand cradled the mussed head as he drew Davey close. Sheba, the shadow, crowded against both males and nudged Davey with her nose.

"Chief Rainmaker should be here any minute." She set her cup aside. "What will we tell him?"

Kade gazed at her over Davey's shoulder. "That's up to Davey." Holding the child by the shoulders, he eased back to make eye contact. "Why did you run away last night?"

The child shrugged, expressive face worried. She recognized that look. The one she'd seen on

umber of faces over the years. A boy who knew he'd
one wrong and now had to face the consequences.

"Were the Cunninghams nice to you?"

Davey nodded, then pointed, one by one to Kade,
ophie and Sheba. And finally back to himself.

"Oh, my goodness." This little blue-eyed boy was
uickly worming his way into her heart. She went
) the floor beside him. "I think I understand." She
)uched his hair, smoothing a lock that sprang right
ack up. "You want to stay with one of us. With
.ade or me. Is that right?"

A huge smile displayed several half-grown per-
nanent teeth. He nodded vigorously before throw-
ng both arms around Sophie in a bear hug. She
ibbed her hands up and down his back in a gesture
he frequently used with upset students. Touch, she
as convinced, relayed emotion words could never
peak. Davey's small fingers kneaded in the hair at
er shoulders like a motherless kitten.

"Listen, buddy." Kade gently took Davey by
ie arm and turned him around. The small, sleep-
:ented boy stood between the adults in a cradle of
are and protection. "Sophie and I will try. We can't
iake any promises, but we'll try. We want you to
:ay with one of us until we can find your family."

Davey's eyes widened in worry. He shook his
ead side to side.

"I'm getting confused here," Sophie said. "Either
e wants to stay with us or he doesn't."

Kade shot her a look. "Or he doesn't want us t
find his family."

Davey whapped an attention-getting hand on
Kade's shoulder and nodded. Sophie's heart sun
lower than an open grave.

"That's it, isn't it, Davey?" Kade asked. "Yo
don't want us to find your family."

The saddest expression came over the small
round face and tears welled in cornflower-blue eyes
He lifted his shoulders in a helpless shrug that bot
confirmed and confused.

"But that doesn't make sense. Why would he no
want you to find—" At Kade's expression, Sophi
stopped in midsentence.

He had that look again, the one she'd noticed yes
terday in the trash bin. Anger and despair.

His bizarre reaction set her imagination into hig
gear.

Did Kade's moodiness have something to do wit
kids like Davey?

Chapter Six

Shortly after nine, the social worker arrived along with Chief Rainmaker. By then Kade was ready for a fight. Itching for one. Something was way wrong in Davey's world, and hard as he tried not to go there, Kade imagined the worst.

After sharing kitchen duty with Sophie to prepare a decent breakfast for Davey—an event he'd found pleasantly distracting—they'd settled at Ida Jane's Chippendale coffee table with a deck of cards Sophie had supplied.

"I'm a teacher," she said when he'd raised a curious eyebrow at some of the things she'd taken from the oversize tote. "What can I say? Always be prepared."

"Better than a Boy Scout," he'd replied. She'd rewarded his joke with a smile.

Now he was teaching Davey the fine art of War, a man's game if ever there was one. Davey, the little

wart, had quickly discovered the joys of taking hi
adult opponents' lower-numbered cards and wa
amassing quite a pile. The silent, breathy giggle wa
heartbreakingly cute. Cute enough to make Kad
mad all over again. Somebody was gonna pay fo
this boy's pain. The sooner he could get back int
the investigation the better for everyone.

When the doorbell chimed, Kade left his tw
guests to battle for the remaining dozen cards.

"He's staying," he said to the social worker th
minute they shook hands. If the abrupt statemen
shocked Howard Prichard, he didn't let on.

"Chief Rainmaker filled me in on the details
Prichard ran a speculative gaze over Kade's fac
"I'm still curious as to how a little boy who'd bee
here only once could find his way back."

Kade bristled. Was Prichard making an accusa
tion? "So am I, but he did. Ask him yourself."

He whirled and led them into the living room ju
as Davey slapped a nine on Sophie's two. Soph
pretended insult, laughing, and Davey's face glowe
with pleasure. When he saw Howard Prichard, th
pleasure evaporated. He bolted up from his spot c
the floor beside the coffee table and looked wildi
around. Sophie took his hand and tugged. The bo
collapsed against her, clinging.

Kade ground his back teeth in frustratio
"Thanks to your red tape he was up half the nigh
in the cold, and vulnerable to *any* kind of predato

He hoped Prichard had sense enough to understand that predators didn't have to be wild animals. "He stays with me and he stays safe."

Sophie, with more diplomacy than Kade could muster, levered up from the floor and brought Davey with her still clinging. "Why don't you gentlemen sit down so we can discuss Davey's situation? Would you care for some coffee?"

"Nothing for me, Sophie. Thanks." Jesse Rainmaker stood behind Ida June's stuffed chair, his thick brown fingers resting on the green upholstery. He was solid and calm and coolheaded in the way Kade once had been. Stay aloof. Don't let it touch you personally. It's all about the job.

"I'm fine, too. Thank you," Prichard said, waving away her offer as he settled on the sofa.

Good, Kade thought. Much as he respected Rainmaker, he was in no mood to be hospitable. Forget the coffee and niceties. He wasn't letting another kid slip through the cracks.

With a soothing hand on Davey's back and while holding him close to her hip in a protective, motherly manner, Sophie said, "Howard, I'm sure we can work out a reasonable solution to this problem. You've known me for years. My school does background checks on everyone and I've taught in this town long enough for you to know I care about children. Kade McKendrick is a police officer with federal-level clearances living here with Ida June Click, whom you've also known forever. They are certainly capable of caring for Davey until his family is found."

Kade shot her a sour look. He would find Davey's family. Nothing could stop him. But he wasn't expecting them to want Davey back. Miss Optimistic couldn't get it into her happy head that the world wasn't all cookie-nice and Christmas-peaceful.

"I'll take him," he said to Sophie. "You have your job and your Christmas projects."

"As long as he's with one of us." She rubbed the back of Davey's hair as he gazed up at her, listening to every word. The kid was sharp. Had to be to find his way here in the dark. It would sure help if he could talk.

"What do you say, Howard?" Sophie insisted with gentle steel. "Can we work this out?"

The social worker shuffled through a briefcase. Kade's fist tightened at his sides. A boy shouldn't be at the mercy of a piece of paper.

"Chief Rainmaker and I have discussed the situation at length. I also spoke with the foster family. First, though, I'm duty-bound to interview the child."

"The *child* has a name," Kade said with more vehemence than he'd intended.

Prichard gave him a reproving glance. "The chief and I will need to talk to Davey alone."

"No."

"Mr. McKendrick, I'm not the enemy. We all have

Davey's best interest in mind. A man in law enforcement should understand the need for cooperation in these matters."

Sophie's soft fingertips grazed his arm. "Kade, let's go in the kitchen and have another cup of coffee." To Davey, she said, "Davey, these men are only going to talk to you. They are not going to take you anywhere. Okay?"

The kid looked doubtful. Kade bent to whisper in his ear. "I'll tackle them if they try. Deal?"

Davey hunched his narrow shoulders in a shy grin and nodded. After a few more words of assurance from both he and Sophie, Kade scooped Davey up in a football hold and planted him in a chair in front of the social worker. Rainmaker came around front and went to a knee beside the chair. Kade felt better knowing Rainmaker was in the room. Rainmaker and Sheba. With a wink, he chucked Davey under the chin before following Sophie into the kitchen.

Sophie held up the carafe. "Do you really want more of this? It smells like burned rubber."

She'd hoped her statement, though basically true, would lighten him up.

"I'll pass." Kade went to the fridge for a glass of milk, his glare focused on the living room.

"They aren't here to hurt him, Kade." She mustered up her best soothe-the-beast voice, the one she used when fifth graders fought to a point of hysteria. Most times Sophie didn't let anything make her anxious for long, but Davey could be an exception. He was so vulnerable, no doubt the reason Kade was wound up tighter than a double Slinky on steroids.

"Sorry to get intense on you." He downed the milk and then plunked the glass in the sink with a frustrated sigh. "I'm a little edgy this morning."

Only this morning? Sophie stifled a snort. When was Kade *not* edgy? "Davey's blessed to have you in his corner."

He rubbed a hand over the back of his neck, shot a glance toward the quiet mutter of voices in the living room. "You, too." He grinned then, a tiny thing, but a grin just the same. "We're quite the pair of crusaders, aren't we?"

They were. He, intense and cynical. She, the eternal optimist. "We're a good balance. And we both care about that little boy in there."

"Someone needs to."

"Agreed. I have a plan. Want to hear it?"

"There's a choice?"

She made a face at him, even though she was pleased at the humor attempt. Maybe she'd lighten him up after all. "I think Howard will go for it."

Howard Prichard appeared in the doorway. "Go for what?"

Davey scooted under the social worker's arm and rushed to Kade. Sheba scooted in behind him, toenails slipping a little on the linoleum in her hurry to keep up.

"Davey needs to be in school, but because it's only three weeks until Christmas break and we aren't sure how long it will take to find his family, I have a somewhat creative suggestion. That is, if you're agreeable to Kade and Ida June being his temporary foster family. Along with Sheba, of course."

"It's all about the dog," Kade muttered.

Sophie shot him an amused glance.

Prichard smiled, too. "Yes, he is fond of the dog. For a child who can't speak, he can make his wishes very clear. I think we can all agree that the best thing for Davey at this point is to be in an environment where he feels comfortable and safe. From all appearances, that's with one of you. So, if the plan is acceptable to all parties, Davey will remain here temporarily. We'll file this as an emergency placement and take care of the details as we go."

Relief came swiftly, a surprise because Sophie hadn't realized how anxious she'd been. God always worked things out, didn't He? "Other than finding Davey safe in Kade's garage, that's the best news of the day. Thank you, Howard."

"What was this plan of yours?"

"School."

"Yes, school is an issue. With his special needs, testing and paperwork will be required. We'll have to start from the beginning and do a complete battery, including IQ, placement, hearing, vision." He sighed and straightened a conservative blue tie. "Everything."

"Let me talk to my principal. I think we can work this out. With only three weeks remaining until Christmas break, I'm going to suggest that Davey be allowed in my classroom to help with the annual cookie project. At various times throughout the day, the special-needs department can pull him out for preliminary placement tests and make suggestions for after the holidays. I can pick him up each morning and bring him back each evening."

Kade shifted toward her, eyeing her curiously. "You don't have to do that."

"I want to. If it's okay with him. What do you say, Davey? Would you like to go to school with me and have fun with some other kids?"

A frown appeared between Davey's blue eyes. He looked to Kade.

Kade lifted his palms in a helpless gesture. "School's a given, buddy. Everyone goes."

Davey shook his head back and forth and shrugged. The adults exchanged looks. Kade bent to the child. "Haven't you been going to school?"

Davey shook his head no.

"Never?"

Another no, accompanied by a very worried expression in eyes as blue as a cornflower crayon.

Kade's jaw flexed. He blew out a gust of air. "Well, that puts a new spin on things." He placed a hand on Davey's shoulder. "No sweat. Sophie will take care of you. Right, Miss B.?"

Sophie smoothed the top of Davey's hair and let her hand rest there. The once-matted moptop was silky smooth and clean, thanks to Kade and Ida June. "Absolutely. You can go to school with me and I'll take care of everything from there. Okay? I don't want you to worry one bit. It's Christmas time! The best time of year. Worrying is against the rules at Christmas." With more cheer than she felt, she playfully tapped his nose. Davey rewarded her with a rubbery, close-lipped grin. "We'll have so much fun, making and decorating cookies and getting ready for the Bethlehem Walk and the Victorian Christmas events. You're going to love those. You might even want to be in the parade."

Davey's eyes widened at the mention of a parade. He nodded eagerly.

"Well, it's all settled, then," the social worker said. "The pair of you seem to have the situation in hand, so I'll leave you to work out the details. Call me if any problems arise." He handed Kade a business card. "I'll be in touch Monday."

As soon as the other two men left and Davey was busy wrestling Sheba for a chew toy, Sophie said, "I should go."

"Why?"

The blunt question surprised her. "I don't know."

"Then stay." He shoved off the doorjamb he'd been holding up. "Davey."

Oh, right, for Davey. Of course, for Davey. What was wrong with her? "Saturdays are normally pretty full, but I can stay awhile until we're sure he's all right."

"I can't believe he's never been to school. Do you think perhaps we misunderstood?"

"No." Kade made a noise of frustration. "I was hoping to trace school records. Easy to find a person that way. Which means the investigation into his identity just got tougher."

"Oh." She hadn't thought of that. She knew nothing about investigating a lost child or anything for that matter. Police work was off her grid. Where would he start? How would he ever discover anything about Davey's past?

They both stared for one silent, concerned beat at the boy happily playing with the affable dog. When Kade pushed a hand against his stomach—a stomach she knew bothered him when he worried—Sophie knew she would stay awhile. There were two males here that needed fixing and she was a fixer.

"There's only one thing we can do at this point," she said.

The cynic raised a doubtful eyebrow. "What?"

She grinned a cheeky grin. "Bake cookies."

* * *

The place was chaos. Granted, her classroom was *organized* chaos, but noisy and vibrant just the same. Far different from the quiet Saturday morning spent baking cookies with Davey and Kade. Two males, one terse and one mute, didn't generate a lot of noise. Nonetheless, Sophie couldn't get them out of her head this busy Monday as she and her fifth graders began the cookie project in earnest.

Sophie stole a quick glance toward the narrow window in her classroom door—a tiny space surrounded by bright paper poinsettias and shiny red garland—praying the noise didn't seep out into the hallway and disturb the sixth graders next door. More than that, she hoped the principal didn't decide to pay an unannounced visit to her classroom today.

"Miss B., our group estimates eight pounds of flour." The speaker was Shyla, a red-haired girl with freckles across her nose. Her twin, Skyla, listened in with an identical, perplexed expression. "Zoey's group says we need five. Who's right?"

A babble of voices from surrounding groups all tried to speak at once, defending their estimations. Each year she divided the students into cooperative groups with diverse assignments. Set up in pods around the room, they began with math, estimating and figuring amounts of supplies needed for their groups' baking, costs of the goods, expected gross and net profits. The early days were always the most chaotic as kids got the hang of the project. Sophie, of course, loved every minute of it, even though she went home every evening exhausted.

"I think we have a mistake here somewhere, Shyla." She tapped a finger against Shyla's notebook figures. "Look at your recipes. Take the amount of flour you need for each batch of cookies. Multiply times the number of batches. Then divide that into the number of cups in a pound of flour. Remember we're using an estimate here to have plenty."

Shyla's eyes glazed over. Sophie laughed and turned the child toward the screen hanging on the wall. "The data is on the SMART Board. Go. Check your figures. Teamwork, sugar doodle. And remind Trevor I'll need his cost estimate once you're done."

Shyla scooted away, a frown between her eyebrows as she and her twin debated the figures. Across the room Zoey, the local vet's daughter, ran her fingers across braille instructions and spoke to her best friend, Delaney Markham. Sophie's heart warmed at the way the two little girls had latched on to Davey and drawn him into their group. In two hours' time, the blind girl and the mute boy had worked out a simple, effective process of communication with bouncy blonde Delaney as their go-between.

Sophie's thoughts drifted to this morning when she'd picked up Davey for school. He had been nervous and uncertain about this new adventure even though she and Kade had reassured him in every way they could think of. It was hard to know what worried a child with no voice to express his feelings. So far, he made no attempt to communicate in writing either, a fact that concerned both Sophie and the special-needs director.

Wanting to be sure he was okay, she made her way to the pod of four children seated around a grouping of desks. "How are things going over here?"

"Good. We have everything done except our grocery list." Zoey typed something on her laptop.

"How about you, Davey? Everything okay?"

He nodded, his gaze moving around the classroom with avid interest.

"He's helping us, Miss B.," Delaney said. "He'll be real good at decorating. See?" She tugged a drawing from beneath Davey's hand and pushed it toward Sophie. "He's drawing and coloring the cookies so we can have a plan of attack when we start working."

Sophie's heart warmed at the obvious attempt to include Davey. "I knew this team was perfect for him."

She leaned down to hug the girls' shoulders.

"You smell good, Miss B."

"Well, thank you, Zoey. So do you."

The dark-haired girl beamed. "Mom let me use her sweet pea spray."

"Mom" Sophie knew was actually her step-mother, Cheyenne Bowman, who ran the local women's shelter. Zoey, already a strong child thanks to her father, had bloomed with Cheyenne in her life.

"Miss Bartholomew?" Delaney said. "There's a man looking in our door."

Sophie's heart clutched. Biff liked order and quiet. He'd been accepting of her plan for Davey but he was always a little sketchy about her loosely structured activities.

She schooled herself to turn slowly and remain composed as though her classroom was not the loudest in the building. Before her brain could sort out the man's identity, Davey shot up, nearly knocking over his chair, and raced toward the door.

Sophie's heart clutched for a far different reason. Kade McKendrick's brown eyes squinted through the glass. When he caught her eye, he pointed a finger at Davey and raised his eyebrows.

By now, Hannah, the nosy Rosy of fifth grade, had spied the visitor and plowed through her classmates like a bowling ball to open the door.

"Thank you, Hannah." Sophie parted the sea of nosy students.

"Who is he? Davey's dad?" Hannah shoved her

glasses up with a wrinkle of her nose and peered intently at Kade. "Are you Davey's dad? Why can't he talk? Is he really in fifth grade? He looks too little to me."

Davey had Kade's legs in a stranglehold. Kade looked at Sophie with a dazed expression. "You do this all day?"

Sophie chuckled. Everyone asked that.

Irrepressible Hannah hadn't budged. "I'm Hannah. If you're not Davey's dad, who are you? Are you Miss B.'s boyfriend? My mom says she's too pretty to be an old maid, but she never goes out with anyone. Wait till I tell her."

Face heating up faster than a cookie oven, Sophie said more emphatically, "Hannah, please. You may go back to your group now."

The serious tone did the trick. Not the least offended, Hannah returned to her group, but the frequent glances and loud whispers about Miss B. and her boyfriend kept coming.

"Sorry," Sophie said, cold hands to hot cheeks. "Hannah is a gossip columnist in training."

"I shouldn't have interrupted." He pointed back down the hallway, his tan leather jacket pulling open to reveal a black pullover. He looked really good this morning, shaved, hair in an intentional muss, and he smelled even better. She'd yet to distinguish his cologne, but she'd know it anywhere. The musk and spice had tortured her, deliciously so, on Saturday and had stayed in her head all day Sunday. A man had no right to smell better than chocolate-chip cookies.

"I checked in at the office," he was saying. "The security in this building is terrible. No visitor's badge. No ID. Nothing."

"Redemption is a safe town. We trust people."

"I don't."

"Really?" She cocked her head. "What a news flash."

He curled his lip at her, more a cynic's sneer than a smile. "How's Davey handling all this…this—" he waved a hand around the room "—whatever it is."

"We're doing our groundwork for the project. Zoey, Delaney and Ross have taken him under their wing. He's thriving, aren't you, Davey?"

Davey nodded, though both adults figured he didn't comprehend the word.

"Having fun, eh, buddy?" Kade asked.

Davey nodded again and pointed at his group. The little girls waved while Ross, as blond as Davey and easily the brightest boy in the class, scribbled away at his notebook. His dad was the town physician and Ross already felt the pressure to succeed. A serious kid, Sophie put him in Zoey's group to brighten him up. No one could hang out with Zoey and Delaney and not have a good time.

"How do you actually bake cookies in here?" Kade asked. "No oven."

"We have some volunteer moms who head up the groups on baking days while the cafeteria ladies supervise the ovens. It works."

"Crazy." Expression still wary and a little dazed, he patted Davey's shoulder and said, "Head back to the group, buddy. I need to talk to Miss B."

Davey clung for one more leg hug before doing as he was told.

"He's adjusting," she said, gaze following Davey until he settled again. As she turned back to Kade, the now-familiar tingle of awareness started up again. She tamped it down. This was her classroom and her students were her main focus, not Kade, no matter how appealing or unnerving. "At first, he was very shy, but now that he knows his little group, he's loosening up more."

"Anyone giving him a hard time about his voice?" From the narrow gaze and hard tone, he might have added, "If they are, I'll beat them up."

The thought, of course, was ridiculous. Sophie couldn't quite envision a grown man, a law-enforcement professional, going toe-to-toe with a ten-year-old. But Kade would definitely protect and defend.

She smiled, glad he couldn't read her thoughts. "Kids are curious, but no one is cruel. They're used to Zoey's blindness and I think that helps them

accept others with disabilities. But just in case, I pu
him with a group of very nice children."

"Glad to hear it." He shifted, hesitated, ther
cleared his throat. "I guess I should go."

He pivoted to leave.

"Wait." Sophie caught the slick leather of hi
jacket and held on as she cast a practiced glanc
over the classroom. The students were working co
operatively. Loudly, but without problems. No nee
for Kade to rush away. Davey was clearly reassure
by his visit. Okay, so she was a little juiced to se
him, too. No harm in that, was there? "Any progres
today on Davey's identity?"

"Nothing concrete. I spent the morning with Jess
Rainmaker. Good man."

"He is."

"He's doing all his small department can do." Hi
expression said that wasn't enough, and she wa
sure Jesse Rainmaker felt the same. A small-towr
police department stretched to have the resource
and manpower for daily operations.

"So, where do we go from here?" Sophie turne
to watch her class while listening to Kade. Grou|
work could go sour quickly without her watchfu
eye. "I want to help, but I don't know what to do."

"I'm getting the word out. Rainmaker's men
when they can, are doing a house to house. I pu
a notice in the paper this morning along with th
snapshot you took of Davey and Sheba." He shifte

again, boots scuffing on the tile, obviously out of his element in a classroom full of ten-year-olds. Dads almost always reacted this way. Uneasy, watchful, acutely pathetic until they'd acclimated. She loved when dads visited. Not that Kade was anyone's dad, but still…

"What about the surrounding towns?" she asked. "I'm convinced Davey is not from Redemption."

"I'm working on that. I have a list of area newspapers to email or telephone this afternoon. Hopefully, with enough publicity, we can dig up someone who knows something."

From the back of the room, a strident voice called, "Miss B., Jacob is not cooperating. He says the cookie project stinks and I stink." The speaker sniffed his sleeve. "I don't stink and if he doesn't shut up, I'm gonna…"

Sophie lifted a palm up like a stop sign. "Stop. Right there." To Kade, she said, "I have to get back to business."

"Need me to knock a couple of heads?"

She wasn't sure if he was joking. "Maybe later."

"Anytime." He backed out of the room. "See you after school."

Davey saw Kade's intention and rushed his knees again. Sophie, already on the move toward the disagreement in the back, figured Kade could handle

Chapter Seven

Kade didn't know why he'd gone by her classroom. Well, other than Davey. He'd wanted to check on the boy, make sure the arrangement was working out. But he could have called.

No. Better to see for himself.

He groaned. He'd never been one to second-guess every decision. He'd been decisive, sure, confident.

Before.

But wasn't that part of the reason his department had sent him to a shrink and put him on extended leave? He'd lost his confidence and with it the edge needed to do what he did.

He snicked the lock on his car, the cherry-red paint job bright and shiny in the cold sunshine.

Who was he trying to fool? After a discouraging morning of following dead ends, he'd wanted to look into Sophie's clear, pure eyes, listen to her soothing voice and try to believe that life wasn't always ugly. With her optimism, she had almost convinced him on Saturday that Davey was simply a lost child and some frantic mother was desperately searching for him. Cold reality had struck him between the eyes in the police chief's office this morning. No one in the state was looking for a blond, blue-eyed boy with no voice.

Still, Saturday had been…nice. Over a batch of lopsided sugar cookies, formed into shapes without benefit of fancy cutters, Kade had spent a few hours of peace.

The kicker had come when she'd asked him and Davey to church. To her credit, she'd taken his refusal in stride just as she'd done the first time she had tried to sell him cookies, as if she knew she'd win in the end. She wouldn't. He didn't belong in church anymore, but Davey had gone with her and had come home with a red Kool-Aid ring around his happy mouth and a colored picture of the baby Jesus. The kid was bursting with pride that left Kade with no choice. He'd taped the purple Jesus to the refrigerator.

A cloud moved over the pale sun, casting a weak shadow. A piece of notebook paper somersaulted across the street to catch in the chain-link fence surrounding the school. In this quiet residential neighborhood, cars motored slowly past, a dog trotted toward the playground and from somewhere he heard the buzz of a chain saw.

People went about the daily business of life oblivious to the lurking danger.

He'd been trained to see it, trained to a paranoia without which he would be dead. A week ago, he wouldn't have cared one way or the other. But now—now, he had a purpose named Davey.

Sophie's soft expression flashed behind his eyelids.

One hand on the open car door, Kade squinted back at the elementary school. No gate secured the building from the street, and the school was wide-open, not a security guard anywhere. Anyone could walk in there and execute a tragedy in a matter of seconds. Didn't these small-town people watch the news?

A bell rang and the double doors burst open, spewing out a running, shoving mass of very small children who barreled toward the playground behind the school. Two teachers, neither of them Sophie, followed the pack. One spotted him and said something to the other. He waited to see if either would accost him, demand his name and business. After a moment of staring, they huddled closer into their coats and disappeared around the corner.

Frustrated, he slammed his car door, jabbed the lock remote and headed back inside the school building. Davey and Sophie were in this place. The principal, whoever he was, was about to get a crash course in safety.

* * *

Sophie rubbed her hands over her face and took a deep, cleansing breath. She was tired. Good tired. Today had gone well and each group was ready to move forward with the shopping segment of the project. Carefully organized folders filled with data, shopping lists and cost estimates waited on the back shelf for the volunteer mothers who would do the actual shopping.

The stapler *click-clacked* as she added a candy-cane border to the green butcher-papered bulletin board. Except for this last board, she almost had her classroom covered in Christmas decorations. The students had helped, of course, adding their art-work to the room. Shiny red garland draped from corner to corner. Multicolored lights chased one another around the door and window. Mercy Me's Christmas CD spun out a version of "The Little Drummer Boy."

She sighed. Life was good.

A hand tugged on her arm. She looked down into Davey's enormous blue eyes. He pointed at her face and pulled down the corners of his mouth.

"No, I'm not sad. Just tired." She smiled to prove as much.

The kids had made paper elves to hang from hooks on the ceiling and the accordion-pleated legs bounced up and down every time the heater ac-tivated. They made her smile. Everything in this room filled her with happiness. She could never be sad here. Tired, yes. Sad, never.

"You know something, Davey?"

His eyebrows arched in question.

"You're a very nice boy. Being sensitive to other people's feelings is a wonderful gift. You have that."

He returned the smile and without being asked began to pick up the stray bits of green paper she'd dropped.

Regardless of Kade's suspicions that Davey had been abused or come from a terrible background, Sophie saw signs that someone had taught him well. She'd studied abused children, had encountered some, too, and he didn't fit the mold.

But then, as Kade said, she was an optimist who believed the best.

Kade. Seeing him had stirred up the memory of last Saturday and she'd been distracted more than once today thinking about him. They'd baked cookies with Davey, and when the child wandered into the backyard to play Frisbee with Sheba, Sophie had lingered longer than she should have. Long enough to know she liked more about Kade McKendrick than his crisp good looks.

Beneath the aloof demeanor lived a good person with a powerful sense of justice. He'd find a way to help Davey.

Finishing touches on the bulletin board complete, she unplugged the cinnamon-scented candle warmer and reached inside a file cabinet for her handbag. A knock sounded at her door. A silly, surprising hope leaped to the fore. Kade? Come to retrieve Davey?

"Come in."

Biff Gruber, as tidy as he'd been eight hours ago, stepped into the room. "Sophie, I'm glad you're still here."

"You just caught me." Vaguely disappointed, she forced a friendly look. She hoped he hadn't come to complain about the noise. "How was your day? I saw the fourth-grade teacher hauling Marcus Prine toward your office after lunch."

Biff's eyes crinkled. "I earn my paycheck with Marcus and his mother."

"Roberta rushed to defend him, I suppose." Roberta Prine, a main-street beautician, gossip and all-round trouble stirrer, was raising two sons much like herself.

"Yes, but Roberta's visit isn't what I want to discuss with you." His tone went serious and he got that stiff I'm-the-principal look. "I am concerned about your friends who pay unexpected visits to school."

Uh-oh. She set down her handbag and stood behind the desk, glad for the three feet of distance between herself and her supervisor. This was her safe zone, the spot she chose when dealing with prickly parents.

"If you are referring to Mr. McKendrick, who

topped in to see how things were going with Davey, he checked in at the office."

"His classroom visit is not what I wanted to discuss, although from reports he may have overstayed his time limit. Really, Sophie, the classroom is not the place to entertain male guests."

Sophie bristled. "Biff! I can't believe you said such a thing. You know me better than that."

"Yes, well." He jerked his cuff. "Mr. McKendrick seems unduly concerned with your safety and welfare. He barged into my office complaining about the lack of appropriate security and explained how he could have wiped out the entire student body in seventeen seconds."

Sophie's lips quivered. She pressed them in, bit down hard for a second to stifle the laugh. Biff was not in a laughing mood. "He said that? Seventeen seconds?"

"Something to that effect. I was momentarily stunned after he charged in like a ninja."

Oh, no, she *was* going to laugh. Please, Lord, hold me back. "He is rather ninjalike, isn't he?"

"This is not amusing, Sophie. I run a tight ship and we ascribe to the safe schools' programs. We have policies in place to secure our students' welfare in every area of the campus."

"Kade is in law enforcement, Biff. Perhaps he had some useful ideas?"

"Well, yes," Biff conceded, though she could tell

he didn't want to. "We can always improve. Every
school can, not just us. But frankly, I didn't appre
ciate the man's attitude."

Sophie had seen Kade's attitude in action. "I'm
sorry. He can be a little...foreboding."

His gaze snapped to hers. "Are you seeing him?"

Sophie blinked, more than a little surprised. Was
that what this conversation was really about?

Respectfully, softly, she said, "As my superviso
I'm not sure you have the right to ask me that."

Biff relaxed his stance, his gaze searching hers
intently. "What about as your friend, Sophie? You
have to know I'm interested in you."

A sharp pain started behind her eyes. Sophie
fought down the urge to rub the spot. "You're my
principal, Biff. It wouldn't seem right."

"There are no rules in our school against dating
a colleague."

Biff would know the rules. In fact, he'd probably
scanned the handbook and ethical-conduct form
before coming to her classroom. Now, what could
she say?

"You're a wonderful principal, Biff, and I respec
you tremendously..."

A hint of color appeared on his cheekbones
"Apparently, I've spoken too soon. I've made you
uncomfortable."

She inclined her head. He certainly had. "Thank
you for understanding."

"Yes, of course." He glanced around at the vibrant display of all things Christmas, stiff, embarrassed and probably hurt. Sophie did not like to see anyone hurt, and she had the awful need to make him feel better. He was a fine man. She had nothing against him. But he wasn't...Kade.

Oh, dear. How had Kade McKendrick invaded her life with such rapid ease?

"Your classroom looks festive," Biff said just as Mercy Me kicked into "Winter Wonderland."

"Thank you. The kids and I enjoy it." She fiddled with the straps on her purse, hoping he'd leave before her internal fixer said something she'd regret. All the while, her head whirled with thoughts of Kade. What if they *were* seeing each other? How would she feel about that?

"The new boy is doing all right, I suppose?" Biff asked, apparently in no rush to leave. Or maybe he, too, wanted to mend fences and part on a positive note.

Davey, carefully cutting a paper snowflake the way she'd taught him, seemed oblivious to the adult conversation. She was glad. This whole scenario was embarrassing enough as it was.

"Very well. He's a nice child. A little sad at times, though that's to be expected given his strange circumstances," she said. "He's no trouble at all, and I think my class of natural mother hens is exactly the right group for him."

"This arrangement in your classroom is only tem porary until he's tested and placed."

She tilted her head in agreement. They'd dis cussed Davey's placement in detail. Why did he fee the need to beat a dead horse?

"By then, he'll be more comfortable, I'm sure. O we'll have found his family." She refused to conside that he might have no family, as Kade seemed t think.

"The special-needs director suggested he see a ear, nose and throat doctor."

"I'll pass that information on to his socia worker," she said. "The holidays may interfere wit appointments until after the New Year."

"Understandable." Biff studied Davey with pro fessional concern. "He's certainly an interesting case."

Davey wasn't a case to her. He was a helpless vulnerable little boy who'd stolen her heart th moment she'd seen him clutching a day-old ham burger.

"Speaking of holidays, Sophie, I know you're heavily involved in the upcoming community event as well as spending time with Davey. Are you sur you have time for the cookie project this year?"

A little warning bell jingled. "Are there still com plaints?"

"I'm afraid so."

She bit back a frustrated groan and tried to joke. "Maybe if I baked this Scrooge a batch of cookies?"

"Probably wouldn't hurt." Biff allowed a smile. "I should let you get home. Your father left an hour ago."

Sophie relaxed at his friendlier tone. Somehow she'd managed to soothe his ruffled ego, and for that she was thankful. "That's because I've already decorated Dad's classroom." She picked up a stack of papers and her handbag. "Are you ready, Davey? Sheba's probably missing you a lot by now."

The little boy bolted upright with an eager nod.

Sophie came out from behind her desk and clicked off the CD player.

"Sheba is Kade's dog," she explained to Biff. "Davey's crazy about her."

"A boy and a dog are a match made in heaven." The principal touched her elbow. "I'll walk you to your car."

At the risk of completely alienating her principal, she didn't argue. After all, he was walking her to the car, not asking her to marry him.

They were almost to the door when a golden dog streaked inside the classroom followed by a lean, athletic form. Sophie didn't have a thing to feel guilty about, but with Biff's fingers tight on her elbow and Kade glaring like the grim reaper, she blushed anyway.

* * *

"Excuse me, I didn't mean to interrupt." Kade heard his tone—a cross between a growling dog and a meat grinder—and realized he spoke through clenched teeth. He couldn't say why, but the sight of the school principal in Sophie's classroom set his nerves on edge.

"We were just about to leave." Sophie stepped away from the principal's grasp. "Is everything all right?"

Would have been if he hadn't just been hit with a sharp pain in his solar plexus. "I came to pick up Davey. You're late. Sheba was driving me crazy."

That was true enough. The dog had paced, whined at the door and had dragged Davey's pillow into the living room. The minute they'd barged into the classroom, Sheba had made a beeline for her new charge. Davey had fallen on her neck with obvious adoration. A man could get jealous about losing his dog that way if the sight wasn't so rewarding. Davey needed Sheba in his corner.

"I think you've met my principal, Mr. Gruber."

Kade gave a short nod. "We've met."

"McKendrick." Gruber was stiff as a two-by-four. "Back again so soon?"

"Walked right in." Kade itched to tell the stuffed shirt how easily he'd entered the building with no challenge, no visitor's card, no one to stop him if his intentions were evil.

To Gruber's credit, he only said, "You can be assured, it will not happen again." He turned, again stiffly, to Sophie. "I'll see you tomorrow, Sophie. Good night."

As soon as Gruber was out of hearing range, Sophie said, "You're full of sunbeams this evening. Want to go Christmas shopping? Santa is making an appearance at Benfield's Department Store. You can tell him your wish."

He glowered at her, but he wasn't annoyed. Not at her anyway. Sophie was the bright spot he needed after a discouraging day. Even though he was glad to be focused and working again, he'd hit enough dead ends to make him wonder if Davey had dropped from the sky. "This school is an open invitation to trouble."

"Biff said he's working on it." Jingle bells dangled from her earlobes and a small reindeer pin blinked from her shoulder. She arched a sassy eyebrow. "Seventeen seconds?"

The muscles in his back relaxed. "He told you?"

"About your ninjalike visit to his office? Uh-huh." Face alight with amusement, she hitched an over-stuffed schoolbag over the blinking Rudolph. "You made quite an impression."

"I might have exaggerated a few seconds." He jerked his chin toward the giant clock on the wall. "It's long past three."

She grimaced. "I should have called you. There's

so much to do this time of year. I have trouble leaving on time."

"As long as Davey's all right." And you.

He felt stupid to have been worried, but after surveying the poorly secured building, his mind had run scenarios all afternoon from black-cloaked teens with AK-47s to kidnappers in cargo vans snatching kids from the soccer field.

"He's done well today, Kade." Sophie lowered her voice, even though Sheba and Davey were several yards ahead, bopping down the hall toward the exit. "The special-needs teacher did some preliminary testing."

He slid her a glance. His eyes wanted to stay right there, focused on that sweet, gentle face. "Bad?"

"He has some basic skills, but he's nowhere near grade level. He tests at late kindergarten, early first grade, although we suspect he should be in second or even third."

"Figures." The kid hadn't been in school. Period. Wherever he'd been, whatever someone had been doing with him, academics had been ignored.

By now, they were outside. The wispy, swirling clouds and tempestuous wind threatened a weather change. They made him edgy, stressed, as if a storm was coming and he couldn't stop it.

He hoped with everything in him that the wrong person didn't discover Davey's whereabouts.

"I'm parked in the teacher's lot," Sophie said.

pausing at the place where the chain-link fence opened to the street.

"I'm over there." He motioned needlessly to the sports car parked at an angle next to the curb. She couldn't miss it. Davey was already there, waiting. Kade lifted his remote to open the door and watched as boy and dog clambered inside.

Still, Kade lingered, not quite ready to let her go.

"I'll see the pair of you in the morning," she said, that mile-wide smile lighting her eyes.

"We need to talk."

She stopped, turned, curious. "Okay."

"Do you have dinner plans?" Probably. With Gruber. Although, hadn't the overzealous student in Sophie's classroom said Miss B. didn't date much? Try as he might, Kade couldn't be sad about that little piece of information.

"No."

"We could get a pizza."

Her face brightened. "Sounds good. Pageant practice starts tonight, so an early dinner is perfect. Want to come?"

"For pizza? I invited you, remember?"

Her quick popcorn laugh was exactly the reaction he'd been shooting for. Mt. Vesuvius in his gut settled a little.

"No, silly, to practice," she said. "Tonight is an organizational meeting to determine parts and such."

He sort of knew that. Ida June was building the

Nativity scene at town center where the pageant terminated in some kind of town free-for-all, and she kept his ear full of Redemption's Christmas festivities whether he wanted to hear them. The whole idea gave him hives. What was there to celebrate? A bunch of greedy people making a buck in the name of Jesus? Or the upsurge in domestic violence and drunk driving inherent in the holiday? Give him a padded room first.

"I'll pass on the pageant," he said. "Thanks anyway. Meet you at the Pizza Place."

Sophie tried not to feel hurt, but Kade's abrupt departure as well as his gruff refusal had stung. He'd reacted the same way to a church invitation, but this was different. Kind of.

As she'd driven to the restaurant, she'd had a good talk with herself. Whatever gnawed at Kade had nothing to do with her. She just happened to be in the line of fire. Either that or she was unintentionally pushing all the wrong buttons.

Now, as she sat across from him, downing pepperoni pizza and bubbly fountain soda, she decided to clear the air.

"Why do you get prickly every time I mention Christmas?"

He was in midbite, a string of melted mozzarella stretching from a rather attractive mouth to the pizza slice. Okay, so his mouth was *really* attractive.

Firm, sculpted, with tiny brackets on either side. Davey sat next to him, the towhead barely reaching Kade's elbow in the deep booth. Kade had dropped Sheba at the house with the promise to both dog and boy to save a slice for her.

He chewed and swallowed, an amazing accomplishment considering how tight his jaw always was. "I told you I'm not much on Christmas."

"Why?"

"Too commercial. Crime rates skyrocket."

"I've heard people say that."

He peered at her over his soda. "But you don't agree."

She intentionally shook her head hard enough to make the bell earrings jingle. "Didn't you have Christmas when you were a boy?"

Something passed over his face but was gone faster than Davey's first pizza slice. "Sure. I was a kid. Kids do Christmas. They don't know any better."

She was certain he wanted to say more. Certain there was a "but" at the end of his sentence. But something had changed him, something had stolen his childlike belief in all things Christmas.

"I believe," she said simply.

"In Christmas?"

"And in the reason for Christmas. Jesus."

"Yeah."

Was that a "yes, he believed in Jesus," or a polite acknowledgment of her faith?

She leaned forward, put a hand on his forearm. It was rock-hard with hewn muscle. "Christmas really is the most wonderful time of the year, Kade. So many good things happen. People give more, reach out more. I know there's trouble in the world. There always has been. There were griefs and heartaches when Jesus was born. He faced plenty of His own, but He never let that stop Him from sharing joy and peace and love."

He made a soft noise, not quite a harrumph or a humbug. More of an interesting-but-I-don't-want-to-talk-about-it sound.

"Did you ever read the *Grinch Who Stole Christmas?*" she asked.

"You saying I'm a Grinch?" Was that a sparkle she spotted behind that scowl?

"No, I'm saying I have the DVD. If you want I can bring it over sometime for Davey to watch. Or he can come to my house." There were lessons to learn in that simple Seuss classic.

Davey leaned forward, eagerly nodding.

"Looks like that's a yes." She handed Davey a napkin. "I'll loan it to you tomorrow. I loved the cartoon version when I was a kid."

"Me, too." Kade's admission was almost as good

as an all-out victory. He *had* liked Christmas at one time.

"Christmas at our house was such fun," Sophie said, with a nostalgic smile. "Dad was one of those Santa Claus kind of fathers who made tracks outside our house and jingled bells in the middle of the night. My brother and I would go crazy with excitement."

"Sounds great."

"Yes, it was. The best Christmas we ever had, though, was when I was sixteen. We didn't exchange gifts that year. We spent Christmas Day at the church serving meals and handing out gifts to anyone who needed them." Her heart warmed with remembrance. "I experienced Jesus in a new way that year, and it's stuck with me. I learned giving really is more fulfilling."

Kade gazed at her with a bemused expression. "You must have great parents."

"I do." Or rather did. A shadow passed over the nostalgic mood. "They're divorced now."

She could almost hear his brain cranking out cynical comments. *See,* he was probably thinking, *life really is lousy.* But Sophie would never believe that. Bad things happened, but all in all, life was good and Christmas was better.

"Divorce can't erase those wonderful memories. My brother, Dad and I still talk about them."

"What about your mother?"

"She lives in Tulsa with her new family. I generally see her on Christmas Eve, but it's not the same, of course." In fact, chitchatting with Mom, Edward and his adult children was an evening to endure, not to enjoy. Her brother, Todd, hardly ever came anymore, which made things at Mom's house harder. Mom tried to include her, but Sophie was the fifth wheel, the one who didn't really belong. She'd much rather be here in Redemption with Dad and her friends.

"What was Christmas like in your family?" she asked.

He pushed aside a plate of pizza crusts. Neat little semicircles of leftover bread lined the edges of the dish. Next to him, Davey was beginning to slow down, too.

"Two older sisters. Mom's an executive accountant and Dad's a hotshot lawyer. We had lots of presents."

"Were you the spoiled baby brother?"

His lips curved. "Something like that."

Elbow on the table, she leaned her chin on the heel of her hand, fascinated to think of Kade as a small boy. "Tell me about a typical Christmas at the McKendrick house."

He hitched a shoulder. "Open gifts, maybe go to Grandma and Grandpa's house. Hang with the cousins, play football or torment our sisters."

"I can see you doing that." Which led her right back to the same question. What soured him on Christmas? "Are you going to Chicago for the holidays?"

When Davey stared at him with interest, Kade ruffled his hair. "Don't worry, buddy. I'm not going anywhere."

Kade's gaze found hers and held. She understood. He was here until Davey's mystery was resolved. Sophie appreciated him for that. When Kade started something he finished it, and he did it with a fierce passion.

"Am I being nosy if I ask how you're related to Ida June?" Sophie asked, eager to know more about this man she couldn't get out of her head.

"Nosy? Yes." He softened the answer with twinkling eyes. "But I'll tell you. She's my grandmother's sister."

"Is your grandmother anything like Ida June?"

"If you mean does she drive backward down the street and spout quotations, no. But they are both strong, feisty ladies who can take you down with a hard look."

"You always know where you stand with Ida June."

"Grandma, too. That's why I'm here." As soon as the words leaked out, Kade shut down again. The light in his face evaporated and he shifted uncomfortably in the booth.

"You know I'm dying to ask," Sophie said.

"Long story." Kade wadded a paper napkin and tossed it on the plate. "Ready, Davey?"

Davey slid the leftover pizza and bread sticks into the takeout box and made a petting motion with one hand.

"For Sheba," Sophie interpreted. She reached for the check, but a strong hand trapped hers on the table.

"My treat."

The quiet insistence warmed her. Here was a man whose pride might suffer if she said no. "Okay. Thank you."

Still, he didn't remove his hand and she began to notice the subtle differences in his skin and hers, the long length of his fingers, the leashed strength.

A flutter tickled beneath her ribs. She lifted her gaze to his.

"I should go," she said softly. Regretfully. "Practice."

"Right." He freed her hand, flexed his once before snatching up the check. "What time?"

"You're coming?" She sounded like a ten-year-old elated over a trip to Disney World.

"Davey," he said, pushing up from the padded seat. "He can go."

"I was hoping you'd reconsidered. The pageant is wonderful, Kade. I promise you'll feel more Christmas spirit if you attend." She couldn't keep the disappointment from her voice. He *needed* to get involved. She was sure of it.

"Not this time. Sorry."

Her optimistic spirit soared. *Not this time* could only mean one thing: there was still a chance, and if anyone in town needed a little Christmas spirit this year, it was Kade McKendrick and the mute child he'd taken under his wing.

Chapter Eight

"Who spit in your sandbox?"

Kade slouched in front of the laptop, jabbing keys with enough force to jiggle the table. Ida June stood with one hand on her hip and a chocolate-chip cookie in the other.

Davey was fast asleep, exhausted from his day at school and the excitement of whatever he'd been doing with Sophie.

Ida June poked at his shoulder. "GI Jack saw you eating pizza with Sophie B. You after that girl?"

Sophie. The woman was giving him no peace. Just like his great-aunt.

"Strictly professional."

Ida June made a rude noise. "I didn't think my sister's daughter would raise such a stupid child. 'Who can find a virtuous woman? Her price is above rubies.'"

"I don't think Sophie's for sale, rubies or not. She's all about cookies."

Ida June whacked his shoulder. Cookie crumbs scattered down his shirt. "I'm gonna have to call your mama, boy."

"Tell her I love her."

"Tell her yourself." She slapped a cookie on the table beside him.

Kade closed the laptop with a snap and took up the cookie. No use trying to work with Ida June on him. He'd call his mother in his own good time, when he was ready to give her something besides bad news about her son.

"How was work on the stable?" he asked.

"Slow. I need you back out there tomorrow."

"I can give you a couple of hours." The rest of his hours, both day and night, would be focused on solving this case.

"And then?" The metal chair legs scraped against linoleum as Ida June perched across from him. She stacked three more fat cookies in front of her. "You got any leads on our little guest?"

He sighed in frustration. "None."

"You will. It's early yet."

Much as he appreciated her confidence, he wasn't so sure. "It's as if he fell from the sky."

"Well, maybe he did." She pointed half a cookie

at him. Melted chocolate oozed out in a thick glob. "Miracles happened at Christmas."

Kade squinted at her. "You been in the eggnog, Auntie?"

Ida June slapped the table and cackled. "Life is sure perky since you moved in."

"Yeah, I'm a barrel of entertainment."

"You'll be happier when you get involved."

His great-aunt was pushier than his shrink—a shrink he hadn't called since Davey entered his life. He hoped the agency didn't send out the guys in white jackets to see if he'd offed himself.

There was no use denying his unhappiness to Ida June. She was in on the conspiracy to get him out of Chicago, though like his family, she didn't know the complete story. Even his supervisors had only part of the picture. Fine with him. If he let his mind go there, to what he'd seen and done in the name of justice, he'd be a dead man.

For a while he had been. Then a blue-eyed boy with no voice had given him a reason to keep putting one foot in front of the other. Sometimes the voices in his head said he was trying to make amends, but he knew he couldn't. Not ever.

"I am involved." When Ida June lifted an eyebrow, he went on. "With Davey. He matters." The words sounded angry.

"No argument from me. But he's a child and children need Christmas." His aunt patted the back of his hand with her leathery fingers and rose to rummage around in the kitchen cabinet. "Wherever he came from, whether good or bad, Davey has to be full of heartache. If he's lost from his family, he misses them terribly. If something else—" she paused, drew a breath, the wrinkles in her white forehead gathering in concern "—well, all the more reason for him to grieve."

Kade leaned back in the chair to study his aunt. She was eccentric but also wise. "What are you saying?"

"Keep him busy. Redemption is a loving place at Christmas."

"Sophie's taking him to some pageant thing tonight." His belly started to hurt. He shouldn't have eaten the cookie.

"Good. You go, too."

He wished for an antacid. Or anesthesia. "I'll pass."

Ida June snapped around with a glare. A cabinet door banged shut. "Not and live in my house, you won't."

Or maybe a quick poison. "Blackmail, Ida June?"

She gave him a spunky little grin, like a possum. "Your choice, nephew. You could move elsewhere, but think about Davey. He's just now settling in."

Kade rubbed a hand over the back of his neck. Sure, she was wise, but she was also pushy. He didn't *do* Christmas. Why couldn't the females in his life get that through their heads?

His own thoughts circled around to replay. Was Sophie part of his life now? Did he want her to be? The better question was, could he allow her into a life as messed up and confused as his?

"What do you want me to do?" he growled.

"When Sophie B. shows up to get Davey boy, you just pack yourself right on out the door with her."

"You go. Christmas doesn't interest me." Maybe he should record the announcement for playback at the appropriate moment.

"You're going to deny that poor child in there a little holiday happiness?"

Kade clasped his hands over the back of his head and stared at the ceiling in exasperation. Ida June would not back down. She would not give up. At this juncture, he hadn't the inner reserves to fight her. "All right, I'll go, but that's it. Don't ask me to do more."

"Ask her to help you put up a tree, too."

His hands dropped to his sides. "Didn't you hear a word I said?"

She leveled an index finger at his nose and ignored the protest. "A real tree, too. Not one of those plastic things."

He glowered, hoping to shut her up. He didn't.

"She's a sweetheart, our Sophie B.," Ida June said merrily. "A man couldn't do much better."

Mt. Vesuvius churned to a boil. "I agreed to a Christmas tree for Davey. Leave Sophie out of this."

"You don't think Sophie's pretty?"

Ah, man.

"She's beautiful. And kind and good." All the things he wasn't.

She also lingered in his head like a sweet fragrance, a song he couldn't stop humming. Being around her eased his conscience, calmed the churning in his belly *and* in his soul.

He dropped his head to his hands and rubbed his eyes, tormented and confused. He had no business getting involved with Sophie. But he wanted to more than he'd wanted anything in a long time. So much so that he was tempted to pray. Not that God would listen.

Ida June lightly touched his shoulder and when he didn't look up, she gave him two gentle pats before padding softly from the room.

Davey was a shepherd boy.

A swell of maternal pride rose in Sophie as the towheaded child, along with several others, tried on various robes and headpieces in pursuit of an appropriate costume for the Journey to Bethlehem parade.

They were inside the community center two blocks from the center of town. Dozens had gathered in the wide space for the meeting, some wanting character or singing parts, but most, like Sophie, taking on tasks behind the scenes. The majority of character parts were played by adults, but they'd made an exception for Davey and a few other children. Davey's expressive face was alive with excited pride at being chosen.

Standing next to Sophie, hands shoved deep into his jacket pockets, Kade murmured, "You must have pulled some strings."

"I might have put in a word with the director," she admitted, grinning up into his face. She was still surprised to find Kade here after his earlier refusal.

"How did you get Sheba in on the act?" Kade hitched his chin toward the big dog sitting patiently while Davey placed a halo around her ears and tied angel wings over her back. Catching the adults' attention, Davey pointed at the retriever and laughed his silent laugh.

"Sheba doesn't seem to mind, does she?" Sophie asked.

"She's crazy about him."

"So am I," Sophie admitted.

"I know what you mean. As if he's always been here." And then, half to himself he added, "Wonder why that is."

Since the moment Kade had appeared at Ida June's wreath-laden door behind a spotless, eager Davey, Sophie had had butterflies in her stomach. A few hours ago, they'd been having pizza and getting better acquainted, but she felt as though she'd

nown him much longer than a few jam-packed
ays. In reality, she didn't know him at all, but
here was something, some indefinable pull between
hem.

Maybe their mutual love for a lost little boy had
onnected their hearts.

"Christmas is about a child," she said. "Maybe
God sent him."

One corner of Kade's mouth twisted. "Now you
ound like my great-aunt."

"She's a very smart lady."

"More than I realized," he said softly, a hint of
umor and mystery in the words. "A good woman
worth more than rubies."

"What?" Sophie tilted her head, puzzled. Even
hough she recognized the proverb, she wasn't quite
ure where it fit into the conversation.

"Something Ida June said."

"Ida June and her proverbs." Sophie smiled up at
im. "What brought that one on?"

Kade was quiet for a moment, his gaze steady on
ers. He gently brushed a strand of hair from the
houlder of her sweater, an innocent gesture that,
ke a cupid's arrow, went straight to her heart.

"You," he said at last.

Sophie's heart stuttered. Although she didn't quite
et what he meant or why he was looking at her
o strangely, a mood, strong and fascinating, shim-
ered in the air.

Their eyes held, a kind of seeking for answer neither of them had. All Sophie had were questions she couldn't ask. So far, every time she'd approached the topic of his life in Chicago, Kade had closed in on upon himself and locked her out.

A good woman above rubies, he'd said. Had he meant her?

"Sophie!" Someone called her name from the other side of the room. She startled. Kade's fingertips skimmed down her arm, steadied her and brought her back to the large, noisy room. Then, he stepped away and broke the curious mood. But for a heartbeat of time, the festive noise of Christmas had faded into the background. And they had connected.

Had Kade felt it, too? Or was Sophie in danger of becoming one of those single women who imagined herself in love with every man five minutes after they met?

No, she wasn't imagining anything.

Something deep and elemental had stirred when Kade McKendrick looked into her eyes.

Flummoxed, face warm enough to blush, she forced a light laugh. "Better get busy before they fire me."

The cynical curl of lips returned and pushed her away again. "What's your part in all this?"

"Refreshments."

She hoped no one had noticed her staring at Kade

ke a lovesick teenager. She wasn't a teen and she asn't lovesick. She was…something.

Sophie swallowed down the crazy stir of con- sion. "I'm in charge of concessions. Along with me great volunteers, fifth grade sells cookies, offee and hot chocolate during the event."

Was her voice as strained and tinny as she thought? If it was, Kade didn't let on. Or he didn't notice.

Cookies," he said, amused. "I should have guessed."

Sophie's tension evaporated. Cookies had a way f calming anyone.

"So," she asked. "Which job do you want?"

He drew back, frowning. "Me?"

"You're here." She raised both palms. "This is a eeting of volunteers."

"I'm with Davey." He jerked a thumb toward the ild, who was now shoving his skinny arms into oversize brown robe.

"Coward." She made a teasing face.

His scowl deepened. "Don't push me, lady."

She gave his shoulder a playful shove. He growled d bared his teeth. Sophie wasn't the least bit in- midated. She laughed. So did Kade.

The sound shot straight to her center and settled ke a melody. Happy and light.

Davey heard it, too, and flapped a hand engulfed a too-long sleeve in their direction.

"Better rescue our boy," Kade said.

Sophie nodded, caught on that one troubling, in-

advertent turn of phrase. Our boy. He'd meant noth
ing by it, of course. It was simply a light and eas
term of endearment.

But suddenly Sophie couldn't get the phrase ou
of her head. She'd always planned to have childre
someday.

What would it be like to say "our boy" to Kad
and really mean it?

The next week passed in a blur as Sophie taugh
school, ran the cookie project and volunteered fc
every Christmas event Redemption had to offe
And there were plenty. When he'd cooperate, Kad
came along. He came because of Davey's involve
ment and perhaps because of Ida June's push
ness, but knowing she wasn't the reason didn't sto
Sophie's pulse from jumping or her smile fror
widening.

Her friends had started to tease her about the tin
she spent with Ida June's mysterious nephew. Eve
her father noticed and asked what was going or
All she could honestly say was that she and Kad
shared a mutual concern for Davey. And if the
spent more and more time together because of th
lost little child, what harm was there in that?

Kade was frustrated to the point of fury over th
lack of progress in Davey's case. He blamed hin
self, though Sophie didn't understand why. Whe
she'd asked, she'd gotten one of his black silence

a reply. He'd made an early escape that night, too, now that she thought about it. The "why" in Kade's life was one of his hot buttons. Press for details, and he withdrew.

Sophie considered pumping Ida June about her nephew's mercurial moods, but that seemed so junior high. If Kade wanted Sophie to know about his past, good or bad, he'd tell her.

Yet, she suspected something bad had gone down, either professionally or personally. Something bad enough to leave him wary of letting others close.

On this particular night, with the crisp December air clear enough to see the stars like a billion diamonds against black velvet, Sophie slapped her gloved hands together for warmth and stood outside a makeshift concession kiosk. The Journey to Bethlehem procession wound in slow, stately fashion toward Town Square.

Although her toes tingled from the cold, Sophie's whole body warmed with pleasure at the sight of a very serious and proud Davey following the procession. Brown shepherd's robe flowing, he kept one hand on the shepherd's crook and the other on Sheba.

Beside Sophie, Kade snapped photos with her digital camera and made pithy comments that reminded her of his great-aunt.

He gave a thumbs-up as Davey passed.

A quick smile of half-grown teeth flashed i
reply. Kade snapped another photo.

Watching the interaction between boy and ma
touched Sophie. She saw the exchange of glances
the silent communication. She noticed, too, the her
worship in Davey's eyes and the worry in Kade's
He was growing to love the little boy, whether h
knew it or not.

So was she.

Man and boy. Boy and man.

Davey's section passed, moving on toward Tow
Square. Sophie stood on tiptoe, watching until sh
could no longer see Davey's brown striped head
piece.

Kade lowered the camera and asked, "Can yo
take a break from the concession?"

She'd been working the booth since the tow
began filling with people two hours ago. Her toe
were numb and her nose was as red as her sweate
but she'd sold plenty of cookies with her fifth grad
ers and their moms.

"My shift is over. From the looks of the crowd
people are focused on the parade now. The rush wi
come afterward."

He hooked a hand around her elbow. "Good. Let
go."

A local church choir began to sing "Oh Come, A
Ye Faithful," a fitting song for the entourage movin
in a steady stream down Grace Street. Sophie fe

n step next to Kade, glad for his grip on her arm in
he thick crowd.

Along the route, they passed vignettes of actors:
oseph and the expectant Mary, the shepherds in
he field, the heavenly host of angels, the search for
. room, all ending in the crude stable Ida June and
Kade had erected at Town Square.

Music swelled the night air and filled downtown
with the wonder and beauty of that first Christmas.
Goose bumps prickled Sophie's arms, though not
rom the cold. To her, this night and the retelling of
he birth of Christ was the most special of all Re-
lemption's Christmas celebrations.

With only a little imagination, she could see the
ngelic host hovering above and hear their hallelu-
ah chorus.

The procession would be repeated several times
luring the evening, but the largest crowd came
early and lingered in the town and in the commu-
.ity center to savor the joyous feelings. And spend
noney, as Kade had cynically reminded her.

She'd made a face at him, but his comment trou-
•led her. He was enjoying the evening, she was cer-
ain, if only for Davey's sake.

A familiar woman turned to say hello. Her eyes
widened in speculation when Kade slid his grasp
rom Sophie's elbow to her hand. He tugged lightly,
losing the space between them.

"Crowded," he said by way of explanation. "Don't want to lose you."

She didn't want to lose him, either.

Her eyes watered, stung by the cold, but she felt warm all over.

"Cookie sales should be good," he said.

She nodded, delightfully aware of their joined hands. Although hers were gloved by thick knit, his were bare and strong and utterly protective. She was the safest woman in Redemption. Safe from everything except her own rocketing emotions.

"They already are," she said. "If sales continue this way, our donation will really help someone."

"Chosen a charity yet?"

Her hair rustled against the satiny material of her coat as she moved her head side to side. "No yet. I'm still praying about it." Yet, every time she neared a decision, something held her back. "I think God has something planned. I just don't know what it is yet."

He fell silent, as he always did when she mentioned her relationship with God. The silence hurt reminding her of the one major reason she shouldn't allow her emotions to run amok. Her faith was number one. Yet, she willingly, happily spent more and more of her spare time with Kade and Davey Part of her knew they needed her. Another part knew her heart was getting involved. *Really* involved.

She slid a glance at Kade's profile. The tense

jaw was smoothly groomed, his hair trimmed and tidy, the face handsomely chiseled. But it wasn't his looks, she realized, that captivated her. Although they'd attracted her first, she now saw deeper within to a man who suffered stomach pain and sleepless nights because of some secret, inner torment. But he continued to put himself out there every day for Davey's sake. He'd searched high and low, driven hundreds of miles, interviewed dozens of people. All the while, he presented a kind and caring face to the little boy who adored him and hid his worry that Davey had no one.

Kade raised her camera in one hand and flashed another photo. While she'd been too busy working the concession kiosk, he'd taken Davey to his place on the parade route and snapped pictures of the festivities as a favor to her. Because she'd bemoaned the fact that she would miss capturing Davey's excitement and pleasure.

Even if she'd been trying, it was hard not to care about a man like that.

They rounded the corner and crossed the street toward Town Square. The trees, dressed in colored lights, illuminated the sidewalk leading up to the stable where a spotlight shone on the sweet and ancient scene. The golden light bathed the Nativity in an almost-holy patina. Sophie sucked in a breath of cold air, touched as always by the display. A donkey shifted restlessly while two sheep from Pastor Parker's farm chewed hay under the watchful eye of a golden retriever and a silent boy.

A lump rose in her chest. "Oh, Kade," she whispered.

He squeezed her hand. "Sweet," he murmured.

She'd known the scene would look this way, had even helped set it up, but she'd not expected to feel so moved by the addition of one small boy and his dog.

Davey, with crook in hand, knelt at a right angle to the manger where a small, warmly bundled baby slept peacefully. Mary, beautifully portrayed by the darkly lovely Cheyenne Bowman, kept one motherly hand on the baby's chest. The soft, loving look on her serene face made Sophie wonder how long it would be until Cheyenne and Trace Bowman welcomed a new baby of their own.

Longing pierced Sophie. Longing for a child, for a family, for the man holding her hand.

Oh, dear Jesus. Dear, dear Jesus.

The strains of "Silent Night" drifted from the carolers positioned behind the stable. Sophie swallowed down the lump of yearning and tried to focus on the holy scene.

Kade snapped another photo and leaned close, whispering something in her ear. His breath was warm and moist and fragrant with the candy cane they'd shared earlier. She didn't catch his words, so she tilted her face to his to ask. He gazed down at her with an expression that could only be described as affectionate. Her heart leaped. For a second—one lovely, breathtaking second—she thought he might kiss her. Then, he rubbed his cold nose against hers, smiled softly and returned his attention to Davey.

Sophie savored the feelings that bubbled inside her like a fresh, sweet fountain cola. She was bemused, bewildered and breathless. And happy.

Considering Davey's situation and Kade's high wall of self-protection, she had no business letting her feelings run wild.

But Sophie believed the glass was not only half-full, it was overflowing. And she was overflowing with love for a mute boy and Kade McKendrick.

Chapter Nine

"Dad?" Sophie gave the Christmas bow one last tweak and pushed the red-wrapped gift under her father's Christmas tree. Purchased years ago by her neat-freak mother, who couldn't abide a shedding tree, the old artificial pine was losing its luster. Although she'd regret the loss of the familiar, Sophie had always preferred a real tree.

But the tree wasn't the reason for her visit to the childhood home.

"Hmm?" her dad answered absently. Seated in his favorite chair, he was reading the *Redemption Register* with a pen in hand ready to work the sudoku puzzle on the back page.

Affection expanded in Sophie's throat. With glasses perched on his nose and his graying hair mussed, Mark Bartholomew looked every bit the absentminded science professor. Some called him a nerd, a term he didn't mind in the least. To hear her dad's opinion, a nerd was a pretty smart guy.

"Can I talk to you about something?"

Newsprint rustled noisily as he closed his paper. "Sounds serious."

Still on her knees next to the tree, she twisted toward him with a sigh. "It is."

"I'm all ears." He patted the arm of his chair and smiled. When she was younger, she and Dad had resolved all her childhood and teenage angst with her perched on the arm of his chair. Not once had he failed to soothe whatever dilemma she'd been facing.

Even though she wasn't sure he could help her now, she knew he'd listen. She knew he'd care.

She settled next to him, the padded upholstery thin now over the chair's wooden skeleton. But sitting here again, with the man she'd loved first and longest, put the world into safe mode. "You know the way you loved Mom?"

"Still do." His face was open, honest and a bit nostalgic.

She fought down the protest that always rose when he said those heartbreaking words. Why didn't a man with so much to offer move on and find someone else? Mom had let them all down. How could he still care? Mom wasn't worthy of such devotion.

"I've never been in love before. Not like that, but…" Her voice dwindled away. Dad would understand.

As she expected, he said, "But you're getting there."

"Yes, I think so." She shook her head. "I know so."

"And you're worried."

"Yes again." She leaned in for a side hug. "You're the best dad. You understand me better than I understand myself."

He patted the back of her hand. She noticed, as she always did, that he still wore the plain gold wedding band Mother had given him nearly thirty years ago. She hurt seeing it there, a symbol of one-sided eternal love. They were alike in many ways, father and daughter, and Sophie feared loving as he did. She didn't want to end up rejected and alone.

The thought came out of nowhere. She'd never hesitated to put her heart on the line. Had she? Was she really afraid of love? True, she didn't date much and never had formed a long-term relationship with a man, but she'd consider herself too busy, too happy in her life. Now, she wondered. Had she purposely been avoiding serious attachment until these unexpected feelings for Kade blindsided her?

"Tell me what's going on," Dad said simply. "Would this most fortunate man happen to be Ida June Click's nephew? And do I need to give him a swift kick?"

Sophie smiled, as she knew he'd intended. The idea of her meek Dad giving anyone, especially a lethal lawman like Kade, a swift kick was silly, but she knew he'd try if Sophie needed him.

"Yes, Kade. And no swift kicks needed. Not for him anyway." When Dad raised his eyebrows in question, Sophie admitted, "I don't think he has a clue about my feelings, and the truth is, I can't really explain them to myself. But this is different than anything I've ever experienced. It's like the whole world takes on a brighter color and I can't stop thinking about him and I feel really alive when I'm with him." She made a small derisive sound. "I don't know."

"Poets have been trying to explain love for aeons. But love is from the soul. It's too big for words."

"How can I be in love with him? How can I feel so…" At a loss, she lifted both hands in the air and let them flop to her lap in surrender.

"Complete? And a little rattled?"

"Yes. Yes, exactly," she said. "It doesn't make sense. I've known him such a short time, but I feel like a missing part of me has finally arrived. It's crazy."

"No, not crazy, honey. God wired us humans that way in the Garden of Eden. A woman for a man. A man for a woman. Two parts of a whole unit knit together by God's own hand."

She knew the story of Adam and Eve, but this

was the first time she'd seen the significance. Eve was fashioned from Adam's rib. Eve was part of him and Adam was part of her. God's breath, His love, had joined them together.

And therein lay Sophie's deepest concern. She gnawed at the corner of her thumbnail. A blot of black marker stained the inside of her thumb like the dark blot overriding the joy of falling in love. "Kade's a good man, Dad—"

"Never doubted it. My Sophie's too wise to go for a loser." He made the shape of an L with his thumb and index finger.

Sophie responded to the joke by squeezing her father's fingers together. "But he's not a Christian. Or if he is, if he ever was, he's pulled away from the Lord."

"Hmm. I see. Now, that *is* a problem. Have you discussed your faith with him?"

"I've tried, but when I bring up the subject, he shuts down."

Furrows creased her dad's brow. For him, as for Sophie, shared faith was a no-brainer. With faith in God, anything else could be worked out. "Seems I remember having this discussion with you a while back. Before this got serious."

"He's polite when I mention church or the Lord, but I feel him draw away."

"Then how has he won my little girl's heart?"

"Oh, Dad, in so many ways. The way he loves Davey. He's determined to find the answers to Davey's missing family. His humor, the respect he shows to me." She went on to tell him about Kade's reaction to her school's security. "He wants to keep the whole world safe."

"Especially you and Davey?"

"He hasn't said as much, but I feel it."

"Sounds like he's falling in love, too."

She shook her head. "I don't know. Protecting people is his job and his nature. Maybe I'm just like everyone else to him."

Dad squeezed her shoulder with one hand. "What if you are? What then?"

With a moan, she admitted, "I don't know."

"I do."

"You do?"

"Listen to your old man, Sophie. Love is its own excuse for being. No matter what happens, even if the other person never loves you in return, loving is always a good thing. Love fills you up and makes you a better person every single time."

"You're talking about Mom."

"And you. And your brother. Different kinds of love, but all of them straight from God's heart."

"Oh, Dad. That's beautiful."

"You know what I think?" he asked, tapping her nose the way he'd done when she was ten.

"What?"

"I think you've been mad at your mother long enough. Anger and resentment hurt you, not your mom."

Sophie couldn't hold back a cry of protest. "But she hurt you. And you still love her. You're alone while she went merrily on with her life and a new man."

The bitterness in her tone caught her by surprise. Was she still so terribly angry?

"Do I look or sound unhappy to you?"

"Well, no."

"That's because I'm not. I have a good life, a job I enjoy, friends, a great church family and two terrific kids." Cleo leaped from a windowsill to stare at him as if she understood every word. "Oh, yes, and a bossy Siamese cat. I am a happy, content man."

"I don't understand that," Sophie argued. "How can you be?"

He drew in a deep breath and shifted to cup her face. "I was devastated when your mother left, but a pair of old Dumpster divers came around here every day for a while to remind me that love never fails. Whether the other person accepts it and returns the feelings or not love never fails. They were right, honey."

"How?"

"Doing the right thing by extending love when human nature called for anger healed *me*. The more

I focused on letting go of my hurt and loving your mother no matter what she'd done, the happier I became and the fuller my soul and spirit." He kissed her chin and released her. "Choosing to love your mom was the best thing I've ever done for myself. It set me free."

Tears sprang to Sophie's eyes. All this time, she'd considered her dad as wimpy and passive, a doormat for her mother to walk on. Now, as she compared her feelings for Kade and Davey to those of her father for his family, she finally understood. Even after what Mom had done to hurt her father, he had purposely chosen the higher ground. Sophie had harbored unforgiveness and, as Dad said, the only person she'd hurt had been herself. Her resentment toward her mother and the fear of being alone like her dad had made her wary of finding a love of her own. Then, a battle-weary and heart-wounded cop had leaped into a trash bin, and love had found her.

Sophie slid over the chair arm onto her father's lap for a bear hug. He smelled of English Leather and Irish Spring, the scents of childhood—plain, simple, secure. "You're the best dad in the world."

"Always good to hear." He patted her back. "Did I help?"

"Ever so much." She pushed to a stand, basking for a few seconds in the powerful love she felt for her father and to claim the affection he showered on her. "I love you, Dad."

"Same here, honey."

As she reached for her coat and cap, he asked, "Where are you off to so soon?"

"I have an important phone call to make."

Before she could give vent to her feelings for Kade, before she could trust that love would not fail her, she had a fence to mend. She smiled, anticipating her father's pleasure. "I need to call Mom."

Kade hesitated on Sophie's front porch. He knew where she lived. Had driven past on those nights when he couldn't sleep to make sure she was safe in the little white bungalow. Hers was an older house, probably one of those 1900 historic places prevalent in Redemption. With a small wooden porch complete with cheerful yellow shutters and wooden rockers painted in blue and green, the house was undeniably Sophie's. Bright, happy, joyous. The door wreath was the same. Obviously handmade, probably by her class, the wreath was constructed of recycled Christmas cards cut into leaf shapes and topped with a giant, lopsided red bow.

The sight charmed him. So did she.

A knot formed beneath his rib cage. The thing had started up recently, replacing the burn in his belly, though this was almost as annoying. Almost but not quite. The knot said Sophie was nearby. The woman had him twisted in knots.

He lifted the brass knocker and gave three strong

taps. A sharp gust of wind whipped around the corner of the porch and shoved cold fingers beneath his jacket. Being from Chicago, he ignored the chill. He'd been colder.

He probably should have phoned first.

He waited a couple of minutes, but Sophie didn't respond so he knocked again. Part of him wanted her to open the door. Being in her presence pushed the shadows away and made him feel normal again. More than normal.

The sensible part of him said he should hit the road and leave her alone.

He snorted softly. He was a mess. A certifiable mess. Kade lifted the knocker and tried again. Sophie even had him thinking about his faith, or lack thereof. He wondered if God ever thought about him. Probably not much.

She wasn't home. Might as well move on.

Disappointed, he'd turned to leave when he heard the metallic click of the doorknob.

"Kade!"

He spun around. Sophie, smile as bright and cheerful as a Christmas gift, was framed in the doorway like a picture. She had a pink towel wrapped around her head.

"Got a minute?" he asked.

"Sure. Come in." She stood aside and allowed him to pass before shutting out the swirling wind.

"Sorry I took so long to answer the door. I was washing my hair."

"I see that." He motioned to her head, the scent of wet hair and shampoo strong. She looked pretty with her face scrubbed clean and her eyebrows dark and damp. "Go ahead and do what you need to. I'll wait."

She removed the towel and shook out her hair into a mass of wiggling snakes. "How's this?"

He grinned. "I'm not answering that question."

She laughed, a full, delighted sound. "Smart man. Let me grab a brush and I'll be back."

While she was gone, he glanced around the small, jam-packed living room. Decorated for Christmas, the space sparkled. He could smell the fresh little tree standing in one corner with a mound of gifts beneath it. Nearly a dozen were the size and shape of footballs. Must be for the boys in her class.

A Bible and some sort of book were neatly stacked on an end table next to the telephone and a notepad. A simple silver cross hung above the television. He expected her blatant displays of faith to make him uncomfortable, but they didn't. He felt… comforted. Sophie was Sophie, sweet and real. Her quiet, living faith was who she was.

Where that left him, he still didn't know.

Not ready to go there, nor the least bit comfortable with that line of thought, he resumed his perusal of her cheerful house. His gaze had reached a grouping of framed pictures when she returned.

"There. Tell me I look better." She'd combed the wet hair straight down to touch her shoulders. The color was dark and rich and glossy. Kade secretly thought she would look beautiful no matter what, but he nodded. "Looks good."

Her grin was disbelieving. "Where's Davey?"

"Ida June. Something about GI Jack, Popbottle Jones and a goat."

Sophie chuckled, a motion that crinkled the corners of her eyes and displayed a tiny dimple on one cheekbone. Weird that he'd noticed something that random.

"They have a goat named Prudence," she said. "She's a hoot. Loves people, but has a strong personality. She also makes great cheese. Davey will have fun."

He'd been to GI Jack's place a couple of times. The mishmash of discarded, recycled flotsam and jetsam was interesting to say the least. A little boy would have a fine time exploring. "I thought so, too, though I didn't have much say in the matter. When Ida June speaks I've learned to go with her decision or suffer the quotations."

"I know what you mean," she said, nodding sagely. "Ida June is as much a hoot as Prudence."

"Yeah. Quite a gene pool I come from." He motioned toward the table of photos. "Is that your family?"

"Those are *my* gene pool. The Bartholomews."

"You look like your mother."

"Really?" An emotion, a little sad and a little proud, echoed from that one word.

"She's beautiful."

Her gray eyes narrowed, but her lips curved. Full, pretty lips on a mouth that loved to laugh. "That sounds suspiciously like a compliment."

"It was." Okay, so he'd told her she was beautiful. That was enough. He didn't have to tell her the rest. The only way to keep his sanity and keep her safe was to keep his mouth shut. His gut threatened, just enough to let him know Vesuvius was still in there, waiting for a chance to make him suffer. Keeping things inside was killing him, but Sophie was worth the price.

What had Ida June said about a good woman and the price of rubies? He thought he was beginning to understand.

Sophie crossed the small carpeted floor and detoured around a canvas bag overflowing with schoolbooks to take up a framed photo. "This is the last picture with all of us as a family before Mom left."

Sadness shadowed her beautiful gray eyes. Even now, the separation bothered her.

"Divorce is tough." His parents were still together, but he had buddies who suffered through the humiliation and pain, even though a broken home seemed to go hand in hand with being a cop. Women couldn't take the strain. Or was it the men who buckled beneath the pressure of dealing with the dregs of humanity day in and day out? He had.

He wondered what had happened to Sophie's parents but didn't pry. No use giving her an opening to ask questions he didn't want to answer.

"I was angry at my mother for years," she said softly as she rubbed an index finger over the face in the picture. "Until yesterday."

"What happened yesterday?" There he went, right where he'd vowed not to, sticking his nose in her private life. "You don't have to tell me."

"No, it's all right. I don't mind. In fact, getting over my anger is such a big relief…" Her voice trailed off. She put the photo back on the table and returned to the small couch. A love seat, he thought. A cushy blue-gray love seat that nearly matched Sophie's eyes.

A soft fragrance wafted to him as she twisted one leg beneath her and settled. Either she washed her hair with coconut or the woman was a walking macaroon. Sweet and delicious.

Kade cleared his throat and scooted to one end. Sitting on something called a love seat with Sophie gave him ideas he shouldn't have.

"So what happened?" he pressed, mostly to take his mind anywhere but on clean-smelling Sophie.

Serene and apparently not as affected by his nearness as he was to hers, she told him about the sudden, stunning, unexpected divorce and her mother's secret infidelity.

"She hurt you," he said, anger rising at a woman he didn't even know.

Sophie placed her fingertips on his arm. "She did, but I hurt myself worse."

"I don't get it."

"By not forgiving her. I know it doesn't make sense," she said.

"No, it doesn't. She made the choice to leave. Not you."

"That's what I thought, too. Then. But my dad taught me something. Being a slow learner I didn't figure it out until last night. Forgiveness is always right. My faith teaches that, but I didn't want to forgive her, so I let the anger fester. She wasn't miserable. I was."

Moved by her generosity, he said softly, "You're a bigger person than most, Sophie B."

"I don't know about that, but I do know I feel much better now that I've resolved things with my mother."

"You told her?"

"Yes. Last night, after Dad and I talked, I called my mom. We had a long, honest conversation. When

I told her I forgave her and I loved her, she cried." Sophie plucked at the nap on the love seat. "She cried."

He could see how emotional the issue was for her. She was amazing, his Sophie B. Full of love and forgiveness and decency.

"What about you? Did you cry?"

She looked up, eyes shining with unshed tears. "I did, but they were happy tears that washed away a hard place inside me that I didn't even know was there."

Kade couldn't resist then. He touched her smooth, velvet cheek with the knuckle of his index finger. "There's nothing hard about you. Never could be. You're the softest, kindest—"

He was talking too much. He had to stop before he spilled his guts.

But there was Sophie, gray eyes gentle and accepting, and he felt a wonderful sense of rightness in being with her, here on her love seat on a quiet Sunday afternoon.

"Kade," she whispered, her breath warm against his fingers, "I wouldn't care a bit if you kissed me."

His heart expanded to the point of explosion. He was only a man after all, and he was half-nuts about a woman who'd just asked him to kiss her.

Hadn't he been thinking about exactly that?

He moved in closer, gaze locked on hers, full of wonder and terror and stupid happiness. When his lips touched hers, some of the hard pain inside him melted like wax. She was everything he'd known she would be. Everything he'd dreamed in his restless sleep and waking imaginings. Sweetness, purity, warmth and glory. A fierce emotion burned in him, protective and stunning.

Right before his brain shorted out, he had one sane thought. He was falling in love with a woman he didn't deserve. And he didn't know what to do about it.

Chapter Ten

The next morning, Kade was still reeling in the wild sensation of kissing Sophie, not once but several times. He shouldn't have. He should have cut and run for her sake, but he'd had no self-discipline yesterday afternoon.

He wasn't sure if that was a good thing or not, considering self-control had gotten him into the mess in Chicago. As an undercover agent—a narc—he'd played the part, done his job and lost his soul in the process. Sophie and Redemption—an aptly named town under the circumstances—had stirred a hope that he might actually find his way again.

His cell phone jingled. He plucked it from his pocket and answered. "McKendrick here."

"Mr. McKendrick? My name is James. You don't know me, but I got this number from a newspaper here in Potterville."

Kade sat up straighter in his chair, a tingle of excited hope racing over his skin. Potterville was thirty miles from Redemption. "I put an ad in that paper."

"Yes, sir. That's why I'm calling. I've seen that little boy you're looking for. He and his mama used to come into the grocery store where I work."

"You're sure it was him?"

"Pretty sure. Almost positive."

"Do you know where his mother lives?"

"Yes, kind of," the voice said. "They didn't socialize much, but I remember someone saying they lived in the old Rogers' place a few miles out of town."

"Give me your name again and how to reach you." Kade scrambled for a pen and paper, jotting down as much info as he needed. "Can you give me an address or directions to the house?"

"I think so."

Kade wrote quickly, his pulse pumping adrenaline so fast that his head swam. This could be it. This could be the break he'd been praying for.

Armed with all the information he could pump from the man named James, he rang off and grabbed his coat. On the way out the door, he called Chief Jesse Rainmaker. He had no jurisdiction in Oklahoma, but Jesse did.

Whoever the woman was who had kept Davey under lock and key and then dumped him like a sack of garbage was about to feel the full brunt of legal fury.

* * *

Sophie was beside herself with excitement. Kade had left a message on her cell phone saying he'd had a break in Davey's case and wouldn't be home after school. Would she look after their boy? Of course she would. He knew that. He also knew she'd say nothing to Davey until they had more information.

She touched her cheek, warm from frequent thoughts of the kiss they'd shared yesterday afternoon. Kade had stayed until church time, although he'd never told her why he'd come over in the first place. She'd fed him grilled cheese and he'd helped her wrap Christmas gifts, a hilarious project considering he made prettier bows than she did. They'd talked. And he'd kissed her twice more. Once when they'd been laughing at her pitiful attempt to tie a bow and then when he'd left.

She was still a little shell-shocked by that. Shell-shocked in a very good way. Maybe Christmas had come early for Sophie B.

No, not yet, because when church time had arrived, he'd gone home, refusing her invitation to come along. Disappointed but not surprised, she'd pressed for a reason. He'd given the usual joke about the church roof caving in.

Davey tapped her arm to get her attention. As she handed him the silently requested bakery box, she prayed Christmas was coming early for Davey whether it came for her or not.

A tiny selfish regret pinched her heart. She loved being with this sweet little boy, and she'd miss him terribly if Kade had discovered where he belonged. Although Kade kept his words few and his promises nonexistent, he would miss Davey, too. Hopefully Davey had a family who treasured him even more than she and Kade did.

She ruffled the top of Davey's hair and received his crooked smile as reward. Today turned out to be the perfect afternoon for him to hang out with her after school. Fifth grade had baked and decorated cookies all day.

Being too antsy to remain still, the cookies were a perfect reason for Sophie to keep moving and busy. Even her students had noticed her extra energy and had asked if she was excited about Christmas. She gave them an easy and honest affirmation, but nothing could compare with the gift of reestablishing Davey with his loved ones—if that's what was about to happen, and she prayed it was.

In a chef's apron and plastic gloves, and heedless of the drama being played out on his behalf, Davey stood at a table sorting sugar cookies. Sophie slid each colorful dozen into zip bags and placed them into a small, white bakery box before adding the labels her class had designed—a merry little elf holding a banner emblazoned with Fifth Grade and the type of cookie. Later, she and Davey would make deliveries.

"Just a few more and we'll be finished," she said. "Are you getting hungry?"

Davey's eyes cut from side to side before he grinned sheepishly and pointed at the bowl of broken cookies.

Sophie plopped a hand on one hip and pretended dismay. "Chef Davey, have you been filching cookie crumbs when I wasn't looking?"

He nodded, displaying those half-grown teeth stained with crumbs and food coloring.

"All right, then, my friend, I guess I'll have one of Big Bob's burgers all by myself."

Davey made his sign for Sheba, a petting motion.

"Don't worry," she told him. "We'll go by the house and see Sheba before we have dinner. Deal?"

He nodded, but then his eyebrows came together in a worried frown.

"What are you thinking about?" She tied a strip of green ribbon around the packed box, added the label and the buyer's name. Then she checked off the name on her master list.

Davey moved his lips, though no sound came out, shoved his hands into imaginary jacket pockets, slouched his shoulders and narrowed his eyes in what could only be an imitation of Kade.

Sophie giggled. "You're a little mimic, you know it? You have Kade down pat." He also imitated the preacher at church from time to time and had taken

to flouncing around with lips pursed to indicate Id
June. "I think Kade is making you ornery."

Davey hunched his shoulders in a silent laugh.

"I don't know what's taking so long, sweetie, bu
Kade will be here when he finishes his business
You can count on that."

He could always count on Kade, and Sophie in
stinctively knew she could, too.

They packed up the rest of the cookies and lef
Sophie's classroom. The building was empty an
silent except for the principal's office. When sh
passed by, he spotted her and beckoned her inside

"Sophie, do you have a minute?"

What else could she say? "Of course."

Holding back a sigh, she ushered Davey into th
principal's office.

"Hello, Davey," Biff said.

Davey, eyes wide and intimidated, nodded an
burrowed close to Sophie.

The principal said, "He's getting attached."

"So am I."

He pushed aside a pad of paper and smiled. Thi
was apparently a friendly visit. "You can sit dowr
I won't bite."

"Thank you, Biff, but Davey and I are headed t
Bob's to have some dinner."

As soon as she said the words, she regretted them
Biff would think she was hinting.

Sure enough, he said, "Why don't you let me come along and I'll buy?"

Dismayed, Sophie pressed her lips together, searching for a gentle way to say no.

"Mr. Gruber," she said, holding up the shield of professionalism, "I appreciate the kind offer. Really, I do."

His smile froze. "But?"

"I'm seeing someone." She hadn't meant to say that, wasn't even sure it was true, though Kade held her heart.

The smile was gone now. "McKendrick, I suppose?"

Great. What would Kade think about her announcing a fledgling relationship to the world? "Yes."

"I see." He straightened his shirt cuffs with a quick tug. "Don't let me keep you, then."

"Didn't you want to speak to me about something?" Sophie asked.

"Nothing important." His tone as cold as January, he turned his attention to what looked to be a letter on his desk. "If you'll excuse me…"

Feeling she should say something but not knowing what, Sophie turned to leave, one hand on Davey's shoulder. As she passed through the open door, Biff said softly, "I hope you know what you're doing."

Biff's odd comment nagged at her as she and

Davey headed toward Ida June's to pick up the dog. By the time they'd gotten burgers and fries she'd decided Biff had been showing concern or maybe jealously, and let it go. After delivering several dozen cookies, she and Davey headed to her house where they read and watched a kid movie and kept an ear tuned for Kade's car.

When the boy and dog started to doze on the love seat, Sophie flipped off the television and stared out the window at the silent night. The neighbors' Christmas lights chased each other around the roofline while a blow-up snowman stood sentry on the lighted front porch. Somewhere Kade followed a lead that must have significance or he would have come home by now. She leaned her forehead against the cold windowpane, thinking of him, longing to see him, but longing more to know what was going on.

Please, Lord, let this be a real break, not another dead end that sends Kade into a broody silence and keeps Davey in limbo.

And please, heal whatever is broken inside the man I love.

Kade leaned his back against the cold siding, thankful—so thankful—Sophie and Davey were not with him tonight. Flecks of peeling white paint scratched against the leather of his jacket. He sucked in long drafts of night air, so desperately cold inside that the thirty-degree air warmed him.

He squeezed his eyes closed and rubbed a hand over them, wishing he could wipe away what he'd discovered in the remote, ramshackle dwelling Davey had once called home.

A hand lightly cuffed his shoulder. "Tough thing."

Kade jerked to attention. No use going soft in front of Chief Rainmaker. "I didn't expect this."

"Who would?" Rainmaker rubbed his sandpapery palms together against the night chill. Neither he nor Jesse had jurisdiction in this area, but the county sheriff had granted them courtesy. Already, at his call, a team of investigators crawled over the place, probably the first people to visit Davey's mother in a very long time.

And she was dead.

He ground his teeth together, stomach raging-hot fire. "What do you think killed her?"

The Native American eyed him thoughtfully. 'From all appearances, she died of natural causes. No signs of foul play, no forced entry. Nothing to indicate suicide."

"Just a dead woman and a messy house," Kade said grimly.

"Mostly the kitchen. Evidence that Davey was alone with his deceased mother for some time before hunger drove him to seek food and help."

Kade's fist clenched and unclenched. "I don't like

thinking about Davey alone in this house with a mother he couldn't wake up."

"Nor do I, but empty cupboards and refrigerator, dirty dishes and spilled milk. They all point to a child fending for himself."

"And trying to take care of his mother." Kade closed his eyes again tightly, fighting the images in the woman's bedroom. He desperately wanted to talk to Sophie. Somehow she'd make him believe everything would work out for the best. She would pray and God would listen.

But he didn't want her here to see this. Knowing would hurt her badly enough. "The mother must have been sick for a while."

"Probably." Jesse shuffled his boots against the hard-packed ground. His equipment rattled. "When she didn't waken, he covered her with blankets."

Yanking a tight rein on his emotions, Kade turned toward the rickety front porch. "Let's get back in there. We've got a job to do."

Jesse's thoughtful gaze stayed on him. "You don't have to do this, McKendrick. The county boys can handle it."

"I started it," he said grimly. "This time, I finish."

Rainmaker couldn't know what he meant, but he'd been a cop long enough to understand the sentiment. Kade had something to prove, if only to himself.

"Davey is lucky to have you on this in the first

place. We might not have found her for months without your extra efforts."

A car door slammed and both men looked toward a technician carrying in a satchel of equipment. Trees surrounding the yard shed eerie, fingerlike shadows over the run-down dwelling and the professionals doing their macabre duty.

"Had to do something, though this doesn't help Davey at all." He spoke through clenched teeth, deeply angry at a situation he could not fix. Once again, he'd been too late to make a difference. "None."

"Even as bad as the outcome," Jesse said with quiet authority, "you did an exceptional job. My timing may be off, but let me say it anyway. I could use you on my force. Granted, we can't compare to Chicago—"

Kade interrupted him with a sour laugh. "I'll think about it. Later."

The answer surprised him a little. He had every intention of returning to Chicago as soon as the shrink released him. Still, Jesse deserved the courtesy of consideration.

The two men stepped onto the old porch, a wooden structure about to cave in.

Rainmaker's heavy boots made hollow sounds on the loose boards. "Walk easy."

"And carry a big stick?" Kade asked wryly.

Jesse huffed softly at the humor, a cop's major

protection against the stress that could lead to insanity. "Yeah."

They entered the house. Even though every light blazed and a beehive of uniformed men and woman worked, an empty coldness sucked the warmth from Kade's bones. In his experience, death did that to a place. "Maybe something in this house will give us Davey's full name."

A technician handed them both a pair of gloves. "You know the drill," she said.

Yes, he knew the drill, better than he wanted to. With heart aching for a blue-eyed boy he'd grown to love, he moved through the small dwelling. Davey had lived in this shabby, run-down place. The investigators had to collect every piece of evidence to rule out foul play, but he agreed with Chief Rainmaker. Nothing pointed to homicide. Nothing pointed to anyone living here except Davey and the woman who appeared to be his mother.

Kade stepped on a spongy bit of floor. The weak boards squeaked and gave slightly beneath his weight. "This house is about to fall down."

Jesse, hawk eyes soaking in every detail, nodded. "Can't argue. You going back in the bedroom?"

Back there with the body, he meant. "Yeah. Got to."

Jesse gave him that look again as though trying to see inside his head. Might as well forget that. Even Kade didn't understand, but he felt compelled to be here, compelled to know answers to the questions Davey would someday ask.

A masked and gowned officer, broad as he was tall, shouldered past the two men. "The coroner is on his way. ETA ten minutes." He made a wry face. "Didn't like being woken up. This kind of thing doesn't happen very often around here."

Well, it happened often to Kade. Maybe there was something to the quiet, small-town life.

Wearing the offered masks, he and Jesse entered the room. Several hours ago, Kade had found her. He'd been alone then, with Jesse Rainmaker on the way. He'd knocked, peeked in windows, called out and finally entered the seemingly abandoned house. The moment he'd opened the door, the smell of death had slapped him backward. With terrible knowledge and a dread deeper than the Redemption well, he'd gone inside.

The blanket he'd pulled over her face had now been replaced by a yellow plastic sheet. He'd never found the covering inadequate before. But for Davey's mom, the plastic was too impersonal and cold.

"Did you see the dog?" he asked quietly, gesturing toward the outlined shape of a stuffed animal. "I'm guessing that toy was Davey's favorite, and he left it behind to comfort his mother. He loves dogs."

"Lord, have mercy." The usually unflappable Jesse shuddered. "Grisly situation for a little kid."

Kade had seen worse. Though his heart hurt so

badly for Davey, he wanted to hit something. "The doc said some kind of trauma made him stop talking."

Now he realized his idea of what caused the trauma had been way off. Kidnapping, abuse. Under the circumstances, he wasn't sure which was worse. Davey had awakened one morning to find his mother dead. He'd been hungry, scared, alone. No wonder he couldn't speak.

Jesse's voice was muffled behind the white mask. "Now that we know the cause, we can get him help to deal with the loss. Maybe he'll come out of it and talk again."

Maybe. But maybe he never would.

"How does a kid ever deal with this? How can he erase the memories and terror?" Kade clenched his fist tight, fingers digging into his palms. He would never forget. How could Davey? "Think how helpless he felt. He's a little kid. He could do nothing to stop what happened. Not one single thing."

A flash of young, helpless faces momentarily blinded him. He was projecting, the shrink would say. Forget the shrink. Kade knew how Davey felt, except Kade could have stopped what happened... and hadn't.

Sophie called in a substitute teacher on Tuesday morning. At eight o'clock she was still shaking, though Kade had arrived at daylight with the news about Davey's mother. With Davey still asleep, the adults had sought privacy in Sophie's extra room, a bedroom turned into a study.

Kade looked awful. Unshaved, eyes red and haunted, he looked exhausted to the point of collapse by the news he had to share.

Everything in her wanted to hold him close and comfort him, but he didn't seem to want that. He'd come into the house with his aloof, professional demeanor carefully in place. Now he was perched on the edge of her office chair, bent forward, with elbows on his jean-clad thighs and clenched hands dangling between his knees. His usually polished boots were scuffed and dirty.

"How did he end up in Redemption?" she asked, setting a cup of coffee and a slice of pumpkin bread on the desk in front of him. She was sure he hadn't eaten. Probably not since before finding Davey's mother. "Potterville's thirty miles or more from here!"

"Jesse and I talked about that." Kade cupped both hands around the warm mug but didn't drink. "Potterville is the nearest town to the house where Davey and his mother lived. Back in the woods, down a long, ragged driveway if you could call it that. More like a trail. No reason for anyone to go out there." He looked up. "It's really remote, Sophie. She had no phone. Not even have a mailbox. Apparently she wanted to be alone."

"I wonder why." Sophie rubbed the chill bumps that wouldn't stop shivering down her arms. Kade had to be even more upset by the reality of Davey's deceased mother. He'd been there. He'd seen. And he'd wanted badly to bring a happy resolution to Davey's quandary.

"The investigation into who she was and where she came from should give us some answers about her reclusive lifestyle. Whatever her reasons, she put Davey in the terrible predicament of having no one to turn to when she died."

"He must have been scared and confused," she said, imagining the thoughts that went through an eight-year-old's head.

"We figure he was with her body for several days before he ran out of food." When she shivered again at the word *body,* his hard voice softened the slightest bit. "He probably decided to go into Potterville—familiar territory—for help but got turned around and went the wrong direction."

"Surely he didn't walk all the way to Redemption."

"We think he did." He lifted the cup to his lips and sipped.

"Thirty miles? That could take days for a child who had no idea where he was headed." Days of tramping through dark, scary woods and sleeping in the cold.

Kade's head tilted. He pinched off a bite of warmed pumpkin bread, rolled the moist cake around in his fingers before setting it back on the saucer. Sophie understood. She had no appetite, either. "Now we know why he took shelter in the Dumpster and why he was so gaunt and hungry."

"Oh, Kade. Our poor Davey. What are we going to say to him?"

He pushed the plate away and sat up straighter. "The truth. Once we know what that is."

"It's Christmas. Little kids are supposed to bask in the festivity and make wish lists and eat too much candy, not lose their mothers."

Sophie wanted Kade to agree, and she wanted him to take her in his arms the way he'd done on Sunday. She wanted him to kiss away her sadness and tell her they would work things out for the little boy they both loved. Together.

He didn't.

"Christmas or not, Sophie, he already knows." The chair rollers rattled as he shoved up from his seat and went to the single window. Through clenched teeth, he said, "He always knew. That sweet little kid has carried the terrible knowledge all this time. And he couldn't tell us."

"Oh, Kade." She couldn't stand it any longer. She went to him, slid both arms around his rigid back and pressed her cheek against his flannel shirt.

He gripped each side of the window with a hand as if holding on could keep him from feeling.

But she knew people. She knew him. And he was aching inside.

"You did everything you could, Kade."

"Not enough."

"I can't imagine what you went through last night, but it had to be awful."

The muscles of his back tightened. "It's my job."

"You're a man. With a big heart. Who loves that woman's boy." With slow circles of her palm, Sophie rubbed the tension between his shoulder blades and silently prayed for him.

He went right on staring out the window at the bleak December landscape and said nothing for the longest time.

He wanted to be the strong one, even when he was hurting. He was the guardian, the protector.

"You don't have to be strong for me, Kade," she said gently. "I know you're upset."

He turned then and touched her face, a tender look in his eyes. Her heart filled. She was certain he had something more to say, but his cell phone interrupted.

After a glance at the caller ID, he said, "The police chief," and answered.

The conversation was brief and as he slowly slid the phone into his jacket, he said, "He found something in the house he wants me to see. He says it's important."

Chapter Eleven

Kade knew only one way to tell her. Straight-out.

Adrenaline pumping from the discovery, he drew in a deep breath, leaned both palms on her round dining table and said, "Davey was born without a voice."

Sophie's gray eyes widened with shock. "But that doesn't make sense. I thought only deaf children were born mute."

Kade had been as stunned as Sophie when Chief Rainmaker showed him the fat notebook crammed with wide-rule paper and dark, scribbled cursive. He'd spent an hour browsing through the rambling, sometimes erratic writings.

"Apparently not," he said, voice low. Davey and Sheba were only a few feet away in the small living room watching cartoons. Even now, the zippy music of *Tom and Jerry* seeped through the walls, a contrast to the serious discussion going on here. "We don't know the whole story—and we may never—but at least we have some information, thanks to a journal kept by Melissa Stephens, Davey's mother."

"And she wrote that Davey has never spoken?" Sophie slowly withdrew a chair from the table and slumped onto the seat. "Ever?"

"Never."

Stunned, she propped her elbows on the gleaming cherrywood and rested her chin on folded hands. "I can't quite come to grips with that."

Her hair swung forward. Kade resisted the urge to brush it back, to feel the silkiness on his skin. Duty first. Always.

"Neither could she, apparently." He tugged a chair close to hers and straddled it, too juiced to sit for long. Seeing the pieces of an investigative puzzle come together did that to him. "She wrote long, stress-filled pages about his illness, as she termed it. She had some notion her mistakes had caused the problem."

Sophie turned her face toward him. "What had she done?"

Kade shrugged a palm. "She never said. Maybe she never knew."

The journal's discovery had eased his anxiety, as he hoped it would Sophie's once she'd absorbed the shock. Davey had not been abused or mistreated, at least not in the ways he'd imagined. If Melissa

Stephens parented poorly, she did so out of igno-
rance and fear.

"Appears she worried about everything. Worried
D.H.S would take him away. Worried he'd be bul-
lied at school. She was phobic about her mute son."

"So she didn't take him out into the world. At
least not very much."

"Right. Not even to school. She was terrified of
school authorities, although she mentioned home-
schooling at one point."

Sophie's folded hands thudded to the tabletop. "I
have my doubts about that."

"I think she did her best." He dangled his fingers
over the top of the chair and onto Sophie's forearm
in a light tickle of reassurance. "In her own way,
he loved him, but she was a scared, lonely woman
with no apparent support system. She was afraid to
go out in public, afraid of people."

In a gesture so natural Kade didn't notice in time
to resist, Sophie turned one hand up and laced her
fingers with his. "Agoraphobia?"

So much for duty first. Aw, who was he kidding?
Sophie and Davey came first, no contest.

"Maybe," he said. "Hard to say because she
doesn't appear to have sought treatment."

"What about her family? Didn't she have relatives
to help her?"

"The police are checking into that. Into all her

background for that matter. But the journal mentions no one but Davey."

"That's incredibly sad."

"Yeah."

He squeezed her fingers, letting her in close now that he'd gotten himself under control. Hard as was to admit, he needed this, needed her.

Earlier, when the discovery of the body had been so raw inside him, he'd feared imploding right before Sophie's eyes. He wanted to be strong for her. For both of them.

"You're exhausted," she said softly.

He was tired to the marrow, but there would be no sleep today. Probably not tonight, either. "I'm okay."

She rose and came around behind to knead the knotty slope of his shoulders.

He tensed, the hard knots tightening to the breaking point. "You don't have to—"

"I know," she said, a smile in her voice as she stroked along his hairline. "I want to. Relax."

Relax? When his heart had shifted into overdrive

She karate chopped the top of his shoulders. "I said relax, McKendrick. Don't make me have to hurt you."

Sophie hurt him? He chuckled, and when he did the cords of stress in his neck eased.

"That's it," Sophie said. "Let go."

Let go? He wanted to grab her and never let go

But he kept those random thoughts to himself and let his head fall forward in a pendulum sway.

"You're pretty strong for a girl."

She gave him another karate chop. "Watch it, buster."

He chuckled again and let himself relish the surprising strength of Sophie's fingers against his tight, tight muscles.

Last night's ugliness dimmed a bit. Being with Sophie had that power.

Doing his best not to drool, he dropped his head deeper and deeper until his forehead rested on the chair back. Sophie massaged and hummed while in the living room Scooby and Shaggy raced around saving the world.

He wished it was that easy.

After a while, his neck felt like putty and he fought the urge to doze. Sleeping on the job was not allowed.

Reluctantly, he placed a hand on Sophie's to stop the glorious kneading.

"Thanks," he said. The word came out in an embarrassing slur. He cleared his throat and sat up straight.

"Better?" she asked, coming around to his side.

"Much." He drew in a deep, cleansing breath. Her macaroon scent swirled into his brain. A man could get used to this, he thought. With her around, he'd go soft as a marshmallow in record time.

Right now, he couldn't decide if that was a good thing or a bad one.

"What now?" she asked and the simple question jerked him back to the terrible reality of death and an orphaned child.

"We have to tell him."

"Yes. He needs to know, and he needs our assurance that he did everything he could and nothing was his fault."

Raking a hand over his mouth and chin, he sighed a noisy sigh. Reality stunk. "He has bad dreams."

"I'm not surprised," she said. "I doubt if he really understands what transpired. Those awful days are inside him and he can't share what he knows or fears."

Kade pushed up from the chair, heart heavy with dread. So much for the relaxing massage.

"All right, then," he said. "Let's do it."

The conversation went easier than either adult expected. Davey had known his mother was gone and even though his eyes filled with tears, he seemed relieved when Kade told him he'd done the right things and his mother was simply too sick to get better.

Sophie made comments about heaven and Jesus and how much Davey's mother loved him. Kade cleared his throat a couple of times, moved by her gentle compassion and the way Davey clung to every word. And to Kade's neck.

"She knew how much you loved her, too," Sophie said, touching the place over Davey's heart.

He nodded, fat tears quivering on his pale eyelashes. Kade tightened his hold on the skinny waist and tugged him closer, wishing he could absorb the pain and let Davey go free. Davey's thin arms clung with a desperation that ripped Kade's heart out.

Sheba, with her dog sensibility, nudged close to her favorite child and whined. Davey reached a grubby, nail-bitten hand to Sheba's head. The connection seemed to comfort them both.

The four of them, man and woman, boy and dog, were locked in a circle of grief and love. For all his determination to remain aloof and professional, Kade accepted that he was done for. No matter what happened from here, he was connected by this experience. To these people. Letting go would not be easy. Not now.

Over Davey's head, he met Sophie's questioning gaze. He nodded, signaling agreement. Davey would grieve and process in the hours and days ahead. They'd help him all they could. If there was a chance he could talk again…

"Davey?" Sophie asked, stroking his hair the way he'd stroked Kade's, kneading and tender and comforting all at once.

Davey raised his head from Kade's chest and lef
a warm spot on his shirtfront, right over his heart.

Sophie handed him a tissue from her pocket, and
Kade almost smiled. The teacher was always prepared.

"Have you ever been able to speak?"

The adults knew the answer, but Kade also knew
where Sophie was leading. The sooner they started
the sooner they'd know if Davey could be helped.

Davey scrubbed the tissue over his tearstained
cheeks and shook his head no.

"Did your mama ever take you to a doctor to have
your throat checked?"

The small face screwed up in thought before he
shook his head again.

Sophie and Kade exchanged glances. No big surprise there.

"Add that to your Christmas list," he murmured
tugging Davey back to his chest. For some reason
he couldn't keep his hands off the hurting boy.
Though, come to think of it, Davey seemed to be
handling things better than the adults.

Of course, he'd been dealing with his mother's
death these past few weeks on his own. Amazing
kid.

"I'll call the clinic today." Sophie sat back on her
heels. "Dr. Stampley didn't discover anything amiss
before, but he mentioned more tests. We were going

o see an ENT after the first of the year anyway.
Maybe we can move things up."

If there was any way to help Davey, Kade was all
over it. He'd even pay for the office call. "I'll take
him myself. Anywhere, anytime. Name the day."

She placed her hand over his. "I know. Me, too."

A day with Sophie sounded good, even on a trip
to a throat specialist.

Davey looked back and forth between the adults,
listening intently to the conversation.

"We think a doctor might be able to fix your
voice," Sophie told him.

He cocked his head and frowned before touching
his hand to his throat. To a boy who'd never spoken,
the notion probably seemed impossible.

Kade hoped not. Life had taken Davey's mother.
The least it could do was give him a voice.

Reality, that cruel viper, raised its head and child-
issed. Davey had no one. He was an orphan. A voice
would help, but he'd still be alone in a cruel world.

"And then what?" he murmured, suddenly angry
at the lousy injustice he couldn't control. Not in
Chicago. Not even here.

Sophie shook her head and frowned a warning.
Today was not the time. She was right, he knew, but
he also knew if no relative was forthcoming, social
services would make the decision. Davey would be
lost in the system.

* * *

News travels fast in a small town and by afternoon, the buzz around Redemption reached a leve
louder than the church bells playing carols on the
quarter hour. Popbottle Jones, bundled to the ears
against the cold, appeared at Ida June Click's fron
door. Today wasn't his first stop to check on the
child he'd discovered in his trash bin, but this visi
carried greater import.

Ida June, a dear but prickly friend, welcomed him
inside to a hot, humid kitchen filled with scents he'd
not smelled since his mother was living.

"What is that delectable smell?" he asked. His
stomach, prone to beg, grumbled.

"Mincemeat," she said as she slid a perfectly
browned pie from the oven and placed it on a rack
on the counter. "You have a very good nose on you
Ulysses."

"A wise man does not forget the finer foods o
Christmas past."

"Sit down over there and I'll give you a slice."
She flapped an oven-gloved hand toward the meta
dinette. "Be careful. This is hot. Don't burn yoursel
and blame me. You'll have milk with it, too. Much
better that way."

Hiding his smile, Popbottle shucked his coat and
gloves and settled at the table. "Yes, ma'am, I shall
and will be grateful for both."

Ida June sliced the flaky crust, the rich goodnes

of cinnamon and cloves filling the air as the steaming pie fell apart on the saucer. She set the plate and milk in front of him and then jerked out a chair and plopped down. "I reckon you heard about our Davey's mama."

Popbottle held a fork aloft, waiting for the steam to dissipate. "Indeed. A real tragedy. How is the lad faring?"

"Pretty well, considering he has a funeral to attend and not a relative anywhere to help him say goodbye. Cried awhile last night. Tore my heart right out."

The news saddened him, as well. A child ought not to be subject to such heartache. "Then the rumors are accurate. Davey is alone in the world."

"From all we can tell. A crying shame, too. He's a good boy. Sweet as that pie." She jabbed a finger. "I wish I knew what was to become of him."

"He seems to be thriving here. Perhaps he could remain with you."

"Howard Prichard says I'm too old to take on a handicapped child." She huffed. "Why, the only thing handicapped about Davey is his speech, and if you ask me, silence is golden. The world would be a better place if certain individuals were struck dumb."

Popbottle grinned around the moaningly delicious bite of pie. He felt Ida June's pain. Being considered too old raised his ire, as well. "The only thing old about you, my dear lady, is a number."

"Agreed. I doubt Howard could climb a ladder and repair a roof if his life depended on it, but I certainly can." She flapped a hand in irritation. "I think he's still miffed over the time he was ten and I caught him striking matches behind his daddy's shed. Could have set the whole town on fire in that drought. I marched him right up to the back door and told his daddy. Fred fanned his britches good."

"Yes, well, this time Howard is in charge and he says we're too old."

"You, too?"

Popbottle scooped in another bite of scalding pie. He'd lose a taste bud or two and the proverbial hair off his tongue, but he didn't mind. A hot pie of this caliber was a rare delight, not to be taken lightly.

"Old and unsafe," he said when he could talk.

Ida June fluffed up like a mad hen. That was the thing about Ida. She ruffled easily when her friends were insulted. He smiled a little. Ida June ruffled easily over about anything.

"That is the silliest lie ever told," she said. "Neither you nor GI Jack would hurt a bug."

"Not us, per se, Ida June. Our humble abode. Certainly, I see his point. A recycling business engenders unstable piles of old bicycle parts, bottles, tins, wires, to name a few potentially hazardous elements."

"Perfect situation for a curious boy to use his imagination and be creative."

"Or get injured."

"Well, we have a problem," Ida June said, heavily propping an elbow on the table.

"A conundrum," he concurred.

She shoved a napkin at him and demanded, "Is the pie any good?"

Popbottle smiled behind another forkful. "The best I've had in fifty years."

Ida June slapped the table and let out a bark of laughter. "Well said, my friend. I won't ask how long since your last taste. That nephew of mine won't touch mincemeat, you know."

"All the better for you and me. And speaking of Kade, why doesn't he adopt Davey? He's fond of the child."

"I've been after him about that very thing. Any fool with one eye and half a brain can see he dotes on Davey." She gave a loud huff. "Why, Kade's practically given him that dog of his, and before Davey came along, dog and master were inseparable."

"He's reluctant to adopt?"

"To hear his story, the child needs a father and a mother, not a burned-out cop who might only be around half the time. He's scared spitless, if you ask me. Afraid of loving and losing."

"Rumor says he'll return to Chicago."

"Not if I have a word to say about it." She grinned, a sly, speculative spread of mouth that put a spark of sass in her eyes.

"Why, Miss Ida June, I believe you're up to something."

"Why, Professor Jones, I believe you're exactly correct."

Sophie looked up from her desk to find Ida June Click standing in the doorway of her classroom wearing a visitor's badge on one shoulder of a pair of bright red insulated coveralls. Hair, white as royal frosting, neatly curled from beneath an elf-green stocking cap. Her cheeks were rosy, her eyes were brown and sparkling, and she looked like a character straight out of a child's library book. If she whipped out an umbrella and took flight, Sophie wouldn't even blink.

"Ida June, hello. Davey isn't here. Kade picked him up so I could work late."

"I know that. They're at the house now, racing around after a football in the backyard like two fools who don't know it's winter."

Sophie's mouth curved. Beneath Ida June's vinegary statement lay a wealth of affection. Sophie liked the image of a carefree Kade playing with a delighted Davey. She wished she was with them, but the cookie project and other Christmas functions had thrown her behind on her schoolwork. Grades were due in the office before Christmas break.

"Did you come for your cookie order? I'd planned to deliver later tonight."

Ida June waved her off. "No worry about those cookies, girl. I don't need them until this weekend for the Victorian Christmas."

Everyone in Redemption and most of the state knew about Redemption's turn-of-the-century celebration. Many of Redemption's citizens were heavily involved, including Sophie and Ida June. Sophie was still working on Kade.

"So what can I do for you?" she asked, curious now as to the unprecedented visit from Kade's aunt.

Ida June peered intently down the hallway as if worried about being overheard. Then she closed the door with a snap and marched across the gray carpet, spread her feet in a fighting stance and demanded, "Are you seeing old what's-his-name, the principal?"

Sophie marked her spot in the grade book and closed it. "I suppose you mean Biff Gruber."

"Yes, him," Ida June said, as if speaking Biff's name would give her a sore tongue. "What kind of name is that for a grown man with a master's degree anyway?"

"'A rose by any other name would smell as sweet,'" Sophie answered mildly.

"The Eskimos have fifty-two names for snow

because it's important to them. Makes you wonder about old Biff, doesn't it?" Before Sophie could come up with a reasonable response, the older woman insisted, "Well, are you two an item or not?"

Sophie carefully put her pen in the pencil cup on the corner of her desk. Uncertain of where this conversation was headed, she went for honesty. She wasn't interested in Biff, wouldn't be even if Kade had not entered the picture. "No. We never were. To be honest, I'm bewildered that people keep asking me that."

"Small town, small minds. Two singles working together."

"Colleagues. Nothing more." At least not in Sophie's mind.

"I told Ulysses as much. You wear your heart in your eyes, girl. That's what I told him. And your eyes are looking at only one man. My handsome nephew. Spending a lot of time with him, too."

The room grew warmer. Sophie swallowed but managed to keep her voice even. "Are you matchmaking, Ida June?"

"Well, of course I am," Ida June said with a dash of irritation. "A woman my age has no time for mincing words and waiting on young people to be sensible. Davey needs a mother and a father."

"What?" Sophie's heart bumped. Ida June was moving way too fast. Sophie was still coming to terms with being in love. Jumping to marriage and a family made her head spin. Her heart, too.

"Kade told me about Davey's family, or lack thereof. Not a soul on this earth to stand in the gap for him. No one but you and my nephew."

"And you."

Ida June harrumphed. "Too old to cut the mustard."

Sophie could see how much that bothered the older woman. "Not in my book. You've been wonderful to Davey."

"I can be his great-aunt if a certain pair of adults will cooperate."

"Ida June," she said softly, admonishing, "I'm not sure what you're suggesting." But she had a pretty good idea. If her relationship with Kade moved forward, it would do so on the grounds of faith and love. No other reason. Not even one as precious as Davey could make love happen.

The handywoman clapped a hand on one hip. A tape measure poked out the top of her pocket. "Do you love my boy or not?"

"Which one?" Even though she loved Kade, he had to love her, too, not just Davey.

"Well, both of them."

Sophie pressed her lips together. This was the strangest conversation she'd had in a while, and an elementary-school teacher was no stranger to bizarre talks.

"Kade and I spend a lot of time together because of Davey. We've become good friends."

"Poppycock. There's more between the pair of you than that."

Yes, there was, but a budding love was a fragile thing to be nurtured in private.

Carefully, she shifted the conversation back to Davey. "Social services is still investigating the possibility that Davey has family somewhere. I suppose Kade told you all the details."

"He did, which is why I'm determined to find our Davey a family before it's too late. Before Howard and his cohorts snatch this child away and you never see him again."

So much for distraction. Ida June had a one-track mind. Like Sophie, the older woman had grown attached to Davey and didn't want to lose him.

But what could they do short of something crazy like adoption?

The notion struck a resounding chord in Sophie's head. Adoption? Could she do it? Was she ready to be a mother? Would Davey want her?

The police had uncovered enough information on Melissa Stephens to trace her records. Her story was almost as sad as Davey's. A runaway from foster care, her parents were dead and there were no siblings. Davey's father was unknown. The people of Potterville remembered seeing her a few times, de-

cribed her as quiet and nervous, but no one remembered her having any friends or social contacts.

"Davey's mother led a very sad and lonely exis-
ence," Sophie mused. "Except for one bright spot."

"Her son."

"Yes." Sophie's chest ached for the woman named
Melissa and even more for Davey. "I wish I had an-
wers for you, Ida June, but I don't."

Yet the seed had been planted and she couldn't
top thinking about it.

Chapter Twelve

Kade hadn't been this tongue-tied since he wa
fourteen and his sister's sixteen-year-old friend ha
kissed him at a birthday party. Sophie B. was kil
ing him—softly and sweetly, but killing him ju
the same.

When she'd managed to arm-twist him into serv
ing cookies and wassail tonight at the publishing
house museum and talked about dressing for th
part, he hadn't expected her clothes to affect him
She was always pretty, but tonight she was a ste
back in time, a spectacular Victorian lady in lon
blue velvet. With her dark hair swept up and a tir
hat complete with black veil perched on her hea
Sophie took his breath away.

"Wow," he murmured when he could speak.

Her cheeks turned pink and her eyes sparkle
above the high neckline and cameo broach. "I lov
dressing up for this."

He glanced down at his pressed gray slacks and black shirt. Twenty minutes ago as he'd splashed on Cool Water cologne and checked the mirror, he'd thought he looked pretty good. But now he was plain vanilla to her blueberry supreme.

As he escorted her to his car her skirt swished against the side of his legs. "Are you going to be embarrassed with an ordinary guy from the twenty-first century?"

"Don't be silly. I'm just glad you agreed to come." She slid onto the passenger seat and tucked her heavy skirts with a feminine grace he found alluring. Chin tilted up toward him, she said, "You're going to love the Victorian Walk, I promise."

He held up a finger to stop the *promise* word, but dropped it again when she laughed. She'd made the promise on purpose to rile him. Nothing could rile him tonight. Nothing except his great-aunt, who'd made kissing noises when he told her he would be with Sophie. The old woman was incorrigible.

Ida June had also stirred the crazy thoughts he'd been fighting of late. Sophie B., her scent, her cookie-sweet voice, her gentle ways lingered in his head even when he was arguing with child protective services about Davey's welfare.

Ida June was pushing him to adopt, but what kind of dad would he be? A messed-up, cynical cop who chafed at Christmas celebrations? Davey didn't need that. Besides, Kade was single. A boy needed

a mother. Which brought Kade back full circle t
the woman in the passenger's bucket seat.

He had feelings for her. Big-time. She didn't de
serve that, either.

"How long is our shift?" He put the car in Re
verse and backed from her driveway. The engin
rumbled, but he didn't downshift and floor it t
show off the powerful engine. Sophie wouldn't b
impressed.

"Only an hour. We'll have a fun time, you'll see.

Forget Christmas. Forget cookies and wassail. H
already was, he thought as he drove through th
quiet, radiantly decorated neighborhoods towar
town center.

Beside him Sophie chattered brightly, filling hir
in on local color, including a pretty cool story of th
town's founder.

"Redemption," she said, "was born during th
Land Run of 1889. One day this was nothing bu
prairie." She made graceful gestures toward th
landscape. "The next day, the population explode
with tents and wagons and makeshift structures tha
became a fledgling town."

"Hard to imagine."

"Exciting," she said, sparkling like a jewel be
neath the passing streetlights. "And meaningfu
too. The man who founded the center of town an
bought up claims to make the rest was Jonas Case.

Kade glanced from the road to her, a pleasant ickle in his chest. "What's meaningful about that?"

Not that he cared, but he liked hearing her enthusiastic recitation.

"Jonas Case squandered his youth as a gunslinger. Purportedly, a very efficient gunslinger."

"My kind of man. Be good at what you do."

She made a noise in the back of her throat. "You would have chased him down and arrested him."

"Probably," he said with a smirk.

"At some point, Jonas saw the error of his ways and gave his heart to the Lord. He stopped shooting people and began to preach."

"He was still sending people to meet their maker, just in a different way."

The comment had the effect he'd hoped for. Sophie's laughter filtered over him like rays of June sun.

"I never thought of it that way, but you're right. He was." Skirts billowing over the console, she angled toward him. "Apparently, he had a hard time fitting in, even after he cleaned up his act. People shunned him because of his past."

"Figures."

"So he started Redemption for folks like himself. Outcasts, misfits, those looking for a place to belong, a place to start again in peace and acceptance."

Kade had been enjoying the history lesson, but the

parallels between his situation and the gunslinger'
hit close to home.

"I saw the scripture at the town well."

"'Come unto me, all you who are heavy laden
and I will give you rest,'" she recited. "Jonas du;
the well. He and others engraved the stone as a per
manent reminder of why Redemption exists."

Redemption. Kade ruminated on the word. Som
men didn't deserve Redemption. Maybe he was on
of them.

He fell silent, but if Sophie noticed, she was de
termined to draw him into her celebratory mood.

When they reached the rambling old Newspape
Museum and exited the car, he spotted other ladie
in Victorian dress, cowboys, pioneers, and though
he might as well join in. Anything for Sophie.

He offered his elbow. Sophie placed a glove
hand in the crook, a simple, unaffected action, bu
a fierce protective pride welled in Kade. He migh
not be a gunslinger, but he took care of his own.

He tugged her close to his side, smiled when sh
glanced up. Tonight she was with him.

Dangerous ground, a warning voice whispered

He drew his imaginary six-gun and shot it dowr

When they climbed the tall steps, the door swep
open and a dapper gent in top hat and a long, fitte
coat greeted them. Everyone knew Sophie. Or s
it seemed.

"Good evening, sir. Miss Bartholomew," the man said, doffing his hat.

"Evening, Mr. Martinelli."

Sophie's pretty curtsy and happy giggle tickled the inside of Kade's chest.

"Are we in a time machine?" he murmured next to her sweet-smelling ear.

"Maybe." Her eyes shone light gray, dappled blue and gold by the overhead light. "I told you Christmas in Redemption was fun."

They entered a huge space lit by dozens of Christmas trees. The smell of wassail and pine hung in the air, thick and warm, a welcome respite from outdoors.

"Don't you love those trees?" she asked, motioning with arms that rustled satin and velvet. "They're hand-decorated, homemade, the way they would have been in the early days of Redemption."

She led him to a stately pine adorned with lacy white crocheted figures and then to another heavy with spicy-smelling cookie ornaments.

"Don't tell me you made this one?" he joked.

She sparkled at him. "I wish I'd thought of it."

When she looked at him that way, he got lost. He was out of his element, as if his skin didn't quite fit his bones. All these people, all this decency.

"Christmas was simpler then. More personal and caring, I think." With one finger, Sophie tapped a glittery ball of glued yarn. "Someone's hands took the time to make this. To fill this tree with love."

Kade battled the usual cynical thoughts. Any thing was more personal than mass-mailed ecard and mall Santas who charged to take a kid's picture

But Sophie didn't deserve his bad attitude. Christ mas did seem different here in Redemption. Sure the town glittered and merchants hawked their sale like anywhere else, but there was something els here, too. Something better, gentler, more caring.

That was it, he thought as he watched a smil ing teenager twirl a younger child in an impromptu dance. People cared.

It was enough to make a man want to celebrate

He might even break down and buy a few pres ents.

Astonished at his thoughts, he let Sophie guid him through the enormous old building. They took a while because Sophie being Sophie greeted every one along the way and introduced him until his head swam with names and faces he'd never remember

"Good thing we came early," he said after shak ing hands with a firefighter named Zak and the loca vet. He would remember those two. Nice guys.

"Can't leave you a stranger," she said, and h didn't stop to wonder why it mattered.

Eventually they arrived at the far end of the roor where a section of long tables spread down one wall In the center a giant punch bowl steamed with wha he assumed was wassail, although the smell was suspiciously like apple juice. On either side of the bowl, homemade cookies were piled high on giant platters.

"Fifth-grade cookies?" he asked, mostly joking.

"Some are. The town council bought twenty dozen and others are donated by local bakers. Aren't they beautiful?"

"Can't argue that." The whole place was Christmas-beautiful, though not nearly as pretty as Sophie. She sparkled tonight, more glittery than any gilded ornament. "Let me taste test to be sure."

She poked a cookie in his mouth.

He chewed and swallowed while she laughed at his surprise.

His heart did ridiculous things in his chest.

Whoa, boy. It's only a cookie.

Right, and Sophie was only a woman.

She offered a ridiculously dainty cup of wassail to wash down the peanut butter. He sipped, wondering if he should stick out his pinky and make her laugh some more. He did and Sophie didn't disappoint.

The wassail, however, did. Apple juice and spices. Was that what wassail was?

The trickle of revelers entering the building seemed more enchanted by the juice than he. He found himself dipping and doling nonstop.

Not that he was complaining. A man would be nuttier than he was not to enjoy a date with Sophie.

Together they chatted up the visitors and doled out refreshments. He hadn't talked this much since the last time he'd been on the witness stand and some defense attorney had badgered him for hours. Tonight's conversation was decidedly more pleasant.

Kade was getting into the spirit of the evening when Sophie's principal appeared. Maybe Kade was imagining things, but he had a feeling old stiff-shirt Gruber didn't like him much.

The feeling was mutual.

"McKendrick," Gruber said stiffly, his glance quickly dismissing Kade in favor of Sophie. Kade couldn't fault him for his taste. "Sophie."

"Cookies and wassail, Biff?" she said with more courtesy than Kade felt. What was it about the principal that set his teeth on sandpaper?

"You look lovely tonight."

"Thank you." She dropped a curtsy. Kade wished she wouldn't do that. Not for Gruber anyway. "I see you're into the spirit of Christmas, as well."

Did she have to be nice to everyone?

"Doing my part." Gruber, the peacock, preened in a shiny gold vest. Sissy color, if you asked Kade. A watch chain—a *fob*—dangled from an inner pocket.

Peacock, Kade thought again, this time with more vehemence. Go play in traffic.

But Gruber wanted to linger. Imagine that? "We have a nice night for the festivities."

Kade's small, irritated noise brought a reproving glance from Sophie. He ignored her. Was Gruber a total idiot?

The temperature was freezing.

Painfully agreeable, Sophie said, "As nice as ever." Why didn't she tell him to buzz off?

The overdressed peacock lingered longer, nibbling at a gingerbread man. He nibbled. Not bit. Not gobbled. Nibbled. Daintily. Like a girl. What kind of a man nibbled?

"Your class made these?" Gruber asked, one imperious eyebrow arched.

No, Kade thought sarcastically. Santa brought them in his sleigh so you could stand here and annoy the prettiest woman in the building.

But Sophie the diplomat said, "They did. Aren't they delicious? We've made almost a thousand dollars profit so far."

"Commendable," the principal murmured with a smile as fake as his mustache. Kade had the juvenile urge to give it a yank.

Instead, he showed his teeth in something less than a smile. More like a dog about to bite. "I think someone over there is waving at you, Gruber." *Way* over there. South of the Mexican border.

"Really?" Biff looked to Sophie, whose cheeks reddened and eyes bugged as though she wanted to laugh. When she managed a weak smile, he set his half-finished punch cup on the table and said with a hint of threat—at least, Kade took it that way— "Enjoy your evening, Sophie. We'll discuss your project further on Monday."

When he'd made a hasty exit, Sophie whirled toward Kade with a hiss of suppressed laughter. "I can't believe you did that."

He lifted a lazy shoulder. "Gone but not forgotten. The gone is all I cared about."

"You're terrible." She whapped his arm for good measure.

He rubbed the spot. "Worse than terrible."

She had no idea.

"I have to admit I'm glad he left," she said. "He was acting a little odd tonight."

"Only tonight?"

"Kade," she admonished but she giggled, too.

All right, so he was jealous. Gruber made no secret of his admiration for Sophie. "He's not going to give you grief at work, is he?"

Her inner light momentarily dimming, Sophie caught her bottom lip between her teeth. "I don't think so."

Kade saw the speck of worry. Old Biff might react like a peacock spurned and that would not be a good thing for Sophie.

A growl rumbled in his head. At Gruber *and* at himself. He should have kept his mouth shut.

He was glaring daggers at the faraway principal when a voice intruded.

"Lookey here, Popbottle," a gravelly voice said. "Miss Sophie and Kade is serving up refreshments. I do believe I'll have a taste."

"Apple juice," Kade muttered. "Be brave."

GI Jack, looking as derelict as always, took the offered cup and then slipped a pair of cookies into his shirt pocket. Sophie handed him two more. "I thought you and Mr. Jones were caroling."

"Oh, we are, Miss Sophie." GI swigged the warm wassail and smacked his lips. "Loosening up the vocals."

Popbottle Jones, in an ancient tuxedo and shiny top hat, spoke up. "Speaking of vocals, what is the latest word on young Davey? Has he seen the specialist yet?"

"Tuesday morning at nine we have an appointment in Oklahoma City. We're hopeful."

"Excellent. We'll be praying for a positive outcome. Keep us apprised, will you, please?"

"Of course I will." She handed GI another cup of wassail. Kade figured what the heck and handed over several more cookies. This brought a delighted smile to the old man's grizzled face.

"I knew you were a good one the minute you hopped into that trash heap after Miss Sophie." He chortled, spitting cookie crumbs. "Forty years ago, I woulda chased her myself."

Sophie blushed. Kade laughed with the men. GI was simple but had a good heart.

Popbottle, the dignified half of the eccentric duo, set his cup on the table.

"Caroling commences in five minutes," he said with a doff of his hat. "Thank you for the fine refreshments. Off we go."

GI's head bobbed twice. "Off we go."

"Carolers?" Kade asked as he watched them join an assembled group in period dress.

"Wait until you hear them, Kade. Your doubt will disappear faster than cookies in GI's pocket. Those two are quite the singers."

He knew he shouldn't be surprised at anything about GI and Popbottle, but singing? "No kidding?"

"GI Jack sings tenor, if you can imagine that, and Popbottle has a rich baritone. They're really quite amazing."

He watched her watching them and thought, *You're the amazing one.*

"Do you sing?"

"A little," she said. "Nothing special."

He begged to differ. Everything about Sophie was special.

"What about you?"

"I can wrap my tonsils around a note or two."

"Really?"

"Don't look so surprised. Davey and Sheba think I'm pretty good."

"You sing for them?"

He picked a cookie crumb from the lacy table-cloth, then replaced a few empty spaces with napkins loaded with cookies.

"Pick a little guitar, too."

"That's right. I remember seeing the guitar in your bedroom."

"Sheba's used to it. Stopped howling and covering her ears years ago. Davey wants to learn."

"Guitar?"

He gave her a funny look but didn't say the obvious. Davey couldn't sing if he wanted to. "I showed him some chords."

"Kade, I love this idea. Davey needs ways to express himself. You are a genius."

"The wassail's going to your head," he said, both pleased and uncomfortable at her praise. He played guitar. He could carry a tune. So could half the population. Sharing his love of music was no big deal. It didn't make him a hero. Heroes did the right thing. Whatever that was.

Someone came along just then and interrupted the conversation. The night wore on with cookies and wassail and cold air curling around his legs like an icy cat. The old wood floor was pretty but not too energy efficient.

Through the windows fronting the building, Kade could see a trolley car parked at the corner beneath the glow of lights. An occasional horse-drawn buggy clopped slowly down the cobblestone street. Peaceful, pretty, a time warp.

Carolers, Popbottle and GI among them, stood on the street corners, their Christmas sounds silenced by distance, but vapor clouds and glowing faces sang of joy.

They were sucking him in. Slowly. Surely. And he kind of liked the feeling.

"Have you ever seen anything so wonderful?" Sophie asked, seeing the direction of his gaze.

He turned to look into her glowing face, and he could honestly say, "Never."

Sophie B. was more than wonderful. She was a gift he didn't deserve. Like the town and this night, he felt her moving toward him, opening her generous heart to take him in.

A decent man would go ahead and fall in love with Sophie. He wondered anew how she'd managed to remain single this long. The man who won Sophie's heart would have to be special. He'd have to recognize her for the treasure she was. A woman far above rubies.

There was nothing special about him.

He handed her a sugar cookie, more to stop his thoughts than anything. She bit and chewed, laughing with her lips sealed. Tiny crumbs scattered down her chin. He flicked them away with the tips of his fingers, glad for the excuse to touch her velvet skin.

Sophie sparkled up at him. "Our hour is almost up."

"Yeah?" That surprised him. As she'd promised, he'd had a good time, mostly because of Sophie but not entirely. Redemption knew how to throw a party. "What now?"

He wasn't ready to take her home.

She lifted a mutton-sleeved shoulder. "I'd like to see the living Christmas cards. Want to come?"

"Sure." Even though he had no idea what a living Christmas card was, he helped her into her coat and escorted her down the steep steps to the street, proud to be the man at her side.

Cold air jammed his lungs. He shivered. "Brr."

"Thankfully, there are plenty of stops along the way. All the stores are open. We can pop inside to get warm anytime."

"Like now?"

"Tough Chicago boy." She bumped against him with a grin and then tugged him toward the stoplight on the corner. "The best displays are on this side. If we get too cold, we can hop the trolley to see the rest.

He'd joked about the cold. With Sophie's smile to warm him, he didn't even feel the windchill.

They strolled the streets with the other Victorian

walkers and stopped to peer at Christmas scene
behind the large display windows. In one, a moth
erly woman with an upswept hairdo played the
piano while ringlet-haired girls competed in a gam
of jacks. Behind them a fireplace glowed. A cozy
scene that set him to thinking about family.

A teenage vendor in knickers with a box hung
around his neck ventured past.

"Hot peanuts," he called. "One dollar. Get you
hot peanuts."

Kade fished in his pocket for a dollar and bough
a bag, more for the experience and the warmth tha
the peanuts. And to see Sophie smile.

"You love this stuff, don't you?" Kade asked
handing her the warm bag.

Sophie's face, rosy from the cold, turned upward
"Peanuts or the walk?"

"All of it."

"Yes," she said, happily hugging herself. "I lov
it."

With a catch in his chest, Kade gazed down int
her lovely eyes and thought of how much he'd mis
her if—no, when—he returned to Chicago.

He'd expected the pull toward home to increas
with the boredom of living in a small community
It hadn't.

He found her free hand and tucked it into his
Even in the fluffy, lined gloves, her fingers felt sma

and slender and feminine. A man could be a man with Sophie.

This was a dangerous thought, but tonight was all about pretend. Tomorrow was soon enough to remember all the reasons he didn't belong here with someone like Sophie.

"Is that who I think it is?" Sophie asked when they'd gone barely a block.

An old-time lawman in long, Wyatt Earp duster and black hat strode toward them from the other end of the street, his spurs jingling. Kade blinked in amusement.

"Chief Rainmaker?" he asked when the man approached.

The normally smooth-shaven Jesse tweaked a fake handlebar mustache. "I'm under here. What do you think?"

Kade didn't say what he was thinking. That the look was completely out of character for the staid, professional officer of the court. And he doubted a real criminal would take him seriously.

Sophie spoke up, beaming. "I like it, Jesse."

"Let's hope no one calls me out at high noon for a gunfight. My speed's a little rusty."

Kade had been to the shooting range with the chief. He might not be fast, but he was deadly. For a small-town cop, Jesse was first-rate.

"Did you get my email?" Kade asked.

"Haven't had time today. You find something?"

"A few leads. I think you're right, but I'll need more time to investigate."

Sophie lifted curious eyes to his. "Are you working for the police department on other cases?"

"I've convinced him to use his handy computer skills to chase down some information we need," Rainmaker told her. "I hate computers."

"Kade is wonderful at that kind of thing. Just look at the way he found Davey's mother."

The familiar regret tugged at him. "For all the good I accomplished."

Sophie squeezed his hand. "You gave him closure. That's a lot."

"My office could use someone with his investigative skills and clearances," the chief said. "We're understaffed and underfunded, but I could squeeze some money out of the budget for a man like Kade."

Kade shifted uncomfortably. He was doing Jesse a favor and feeling useful at the same time. But he wasn't working. Not really. Not yet.

The idea of joining a small-town force had him wondering if he was ready to get back in the game. Finding Davey's mother dead had been a blow, but in the end he'd felt better instead of worse. Granted, he'd phoned his shrink to talk things over. The first time in weeks. The shocked doc had made him realize he might be moving forward again.

Come to think of it, he'd slept most of last night and his only dreams had been of Sophie.

He exhaled a vapor cloud. Small-town life was supposed to be simpler, but things were getting more complicated by the minute.

At least for him.

Sophie crunched a salty peanut shell with her front teeth. All the heat had dissipated from the small paper bag, but Kade's gesture continued to warm her heart. He was different tonight. Relaxed and almost happy. The Christmas spirit had overtaken him. How could anyone roam the festive streets of Redemption without being drawn into the mood?

She was always happy at Christmas, although she credited being with Kade for tonight's extra burst of joy. She was in love, and regardless of the outcome, she would enjoy their time together.

She wondered at his reaction to Chief Rainmaker's offer. He'd gone quiet, thoughtful. Was there a chance he'd remain in Redemption?

A horse-drawn carriage clip-clopped to a stop next to the sidewalk and a man climbed out. He reached back for the bustle-clad woman still inside. The woman laughed, threw her arms out wide and fell into the man's embrace. He whirled her around in a circle before setting her feet on the sidewalk for a lingering kiss.

Sophie averted her gaze, pinched by uncharacteristic envy. She wanted to be loved.

A strong hand tugged at her elbow. "Let's take the carriage home."

She pivoted toward him. "But your car is here."

"I can come back for it."

Excitement fluttered. She wanted to. Badly. "It's not too sensible, but…"

The corners of his mouth quivered. With eyes narrowed and a tad ornery, he said, "Live dangerously, Sophie. Ride with me."

Her stomach nosedived. Live dangerously? He was teasing, she knew. The only danger when she was with him was from her own heart.

While she waited in anticipation, he spoke to the driver, handed over some bills and opened the carriage door. When Sophie started to climb inside, his hands came around her waist and he lifted her easily onto the step. She felt light and delicate and protected.

She scooted to the far side of the bench seat and Kade climbed in beside her. After straightening the heavy throw over their laps, all the while fighting down her billowy dress and making her giggle in the process, he tapped on the roof of the carriage. With a jingle of bells, the horse smoothly moved forward.

"How did women manage with all that?" He pushed again, playfully, at her voluminous skirts.

Sophie laughed softly. "I'm glad I'll never have to find out."

"I thought you liked dressing up."

"I do. For one night a year. Every day would be a chore. Do you have any idea the amount of undergarments I have under this dress?" She clapped a hand over her mouth. "Don't answer that."

Kade's laugh rang out, rich and real. To hear him laugh so freely was worth the slip of the tongue. "I'll be a gentleman tonight and pretend I'm not thinking about your undergarments. Those layers must have driven men to distraction."

"Kade!" Heat rushed up the sides of her neck. "Stop!"

He laughed again, dark eyes dancing in the passing glow of streetlamps and Christmas lights. Settling back for the gentle ride, he put an arm around her shoulders and snugged her closer.

"I'll be good," he murmured against her ear, his breath warm and enticing, "if you say so."

"You better," she said, pulse ticking away in her throat.

His lips grazed her ear and she sighed, snuggling into him. The carriage swayed to the rhythm of hoofbeats on concrete, a melody that matched her happy heart.

Being with Kade felt right in so many ways. Did he feel it, too? Or was he just a man saying sweet things to a gullible woman?

No, she didn't believe that. Even though he was a man with a man's feelings, Kade treated her with a respect and tenderness that made her feel more secure than she ever had. They could tease and flirt—and did—but Kade never crossed her invisible line.

As they rolled along, admiring the lights and Santas and Nativity displays, they made small talk. About the celebration. About Davey. About everything except the thing utmost in Sophie's mind. The two of them.

"Look," he said, his voice quiet, "it's snowing."

Sophie gave a delighted gasp and craned her neck toward the carriage window. "I love snow."

"How did I guess? Miss Suzy Snowflake, Miss Christmas Eve loves snow. Imagine." But she could tell he liked it, too.

They turned the last corner and headed down the street toward her house. She wished the time would stand still, that this night would never end, that she could spend forever with Kade, snuggled close in this carriage with the snow falling around them.

The carriage rattled into her driveway. A layer of snow, like powdered sugar on cake, sprinkled the dry grass of her front lawn. The rare sprinkling wouldn't last, would likely be gone by morning, but for tonight nothing could be more perfect.

"Home," Kade said.

She drew in a long satisfied breath. "I don't want to get out."

His gaze caught hers and he nodded. "I know."

They remained there for long seconds inside the warm carriage that smelled of leather and Kade's cologne.

She memorized him, the firm plane of his face, the tiny scar on his chin.

She wondered if he knew she loved him. And she was sorely tempted to blurt the words here and now.

Didn't Dad say loving was always a good thing? Didn't a person as wonderful as Kade deserve to know he was loved?

The driver opened the carriage door. Frosty wind blew snowflakes inside. "Step easy, Sophie. The concrete is a little icy."

"I've got her," Kade said.

The driver, a man she'd known since childhood, nodded and stepped aside. "I'll wait here for you, sir."

Kade alighted first and reached back for Sophie. She was tempted to leap into his arms the way the woman had done earlier, but considering the damp concrete and the risk of a fall, she refrained. Instead, she leaned forward and was thrilled when Kade grasped her waist and swept her out into his arms and against his chest.

"I saw that in a movie once," he said, grinning down into her face. "Always wanted to try it."

She giggled, hesitant to turn loose of his strong shoulders. "What did you think?"

"I think the old days had something on us modern

folks. All these opportunities to hold a pretty girl. Who knew?"

He set her on her feet but didn't turn her loose. Instead he slid an arm around her waist and led her to the front door. Snow swirled around them like wet feathers.

"This is beautiful," she said, turning toward him and the falling snow. "Such a perfect ending to a special night."

"The best I can remember." His answer made her heart sing.

"Ever?" she asked.

"Ever." Then he softly kissed her, the cold snow melting on their warm lips.

When the kiss ended, he cupped her cheek and smiled into her eyes. The urge to declare her love rose like a helium balloon, warm and beautiful. When she opened her mouth to say the words, Kade kissed her again.

Bells jingled as the horse in the driveway moved restlessly. With an embarrassed start, Sophie remembered the driver looking on.

"Your carriage awaits," she said with a soft, breathless laugh.

Kade made a growling sound, but when she shivered, he took her key and unlocked the door. "Good night, Sophie."

"Good night." She started inside but stopped and turned. "Kade?"

He was still standing on the porch waiting until she was safely inside. A surge of love and hope welled up inside her.

"Christmas Eve is candlelight service at church. Will you and Davey go with me? It's such a beautiful, reverent time."

He blinked as though the question caught him off guard. Slowly, heartbreakingly, he shook his head. "Better not."

She studied the troubled expression, the struggle going on behind his eyes, and wanted to argue, but a quiet voice inside held her protest in check.

Lips pressed together, the memory of his kiss still lingering, Sophie went inside and closed the door.

Chapter Thirteen

Kade didn't sleep much that night. Not for the usual reasons, but because of Sophie. Tonight the truth had hit him in the face like a sucker punch. He loved her. He wanted to give her everything a good life had to offer.

The problem was he had nothing good to give.

All she'd asked of him was a church service and he couldn't even give her that. He was a lot of things but he refused to be a hypocrite. He wouldn't go inside a church and pretend to pay homage to a God who let bad things happen to little kids.

Flopping over to his side, he jabbed the pillow with his fist. Ida June's fluffy old couch groaned but didn't give. The monstrosity was ugly but comfortable enough to sleep on—if a man could sleep. And when he couldn't, he could slip out the door without disturbing the household.

Tonight he wouldn't ramble. He'd done enough of that and the bitter weather served as impediment.

Tonight he'd lie here and torture himself with thoughts. He'd hope the ulcer didn't act up, and if worse came to worse, he'd get up and open the laptop. Criminals didn't sleep. Why should cops?

He heard the tip-tap of Sheba's paws and caught the light reflected in her amber eyes as she left Davey's side to come to the couch. Her wet nose nudged the back of his hand.

Kade flopped again, this time to his back. "Need out, girl?"

The dog dropped to a sit and put her muzzle on his chest. Kade echoed her sigh. She didn't need outside. She'd come, as she'd done in those awful first weeks after the end of the undercover sting, because she felt her master's troubled spirit.

Kade rubbed her ears, grateful for the company of a silent friend. Sheba was like Davey in that respect. Gentle and silent.

He groaned again and Sheba shifted anxiously.

Monday, perhaps Davey would get good news from the specialist. Sophie was praying and Kade had his fingers crossed that something could be done for Davey's voice.

Tuesday, a small boy would bury his mother. Supported by Kade, Sophie, Ida June and a handful of new friends, he'd lay his mother to rest.

The implication twisted Kade in two. No one could ever replace his mother, but Davey needed a family. He shouldn't be resigned to his mother's lonely, tragic fate.

The thought of Sophie intruded. Again. She'd been in his mind since the day they'd met, but tonight the romantic carriage ride had gotten to him. *She* had gotten to him. After he'd watched her enter the snug little house and heard the lock click into place, he'd walked through snowflakes to the carriage and thought how much like the snow she was. Soft and pretty, rare and pure.

When he reached the carriage, the driver said it all. "It's a lucky man that's loved by Sophie B."

Did she love him? He thought she might. With all his being he wanted to be Sophie's "lucky man," but how could he be? He was big-city. She was small-town. He was dark to her light and rain to her sunshine. Sophie had faith while he'd abandoned his during a year of asking where God was when kids were being sold to predators, and facing the ugly truth that he was as much to blame as God. He'd been there and done nothing. Maybe the fault was all his, not God's.

But still, a Christmas Eve service with all the trappings and Sophie yearning for something from him he couldn't give.

He just wasn't ready.

* * *

He was ready, however, bright and early Monday morning for the trip to Oklahoma City. He and Davey, spit-shined, combed and overfed on Ida June's pancakes, left the house in plenty of time to test conditions of the roads. Along the way, they picked up Sophie, who insisted on going along. Not that he minded one bit, and her presence soothed Davey, who'd expressed some doubt about being poked and prodded by a doctor.

According to the local doc, Davey was headed for something called a laryngoscope to look at his vocal cords. They'd tried to explain to Davey in simple terms, but all they'd managed to do was make him anxious.

Sophie was in her usual merry Christmas mood, not a trace of the disappointment he'd seen on her face Saturday night. With Davey buckled in the backseat, Kade was tempted to reach across the console and hold Sophie's hand. He didn't, though. Until he knew where he was headed, he couldn't involve Sophie in his life any deeper than she already was.

They made small talk about the Victorian Walk and how she wished the snow had stayed, about the cookie project and the upcoming Christmas break from school. They both carefully avoided the subject of Davey's mother and tomorrow's funeral, but the event played heavily on Kade's mind. After the funeral, what happened to Davey then?

By the time they entered the tall, many-storied outpatient clinic, Davey's quietness had turned to fidgets.

"You'll be okay, buddy," Kade said as he took Davey's hand and led him into the waiting area. "Look, there are other kids here and toys to play with. Look at the size of that truck!"

Davey was having none of it. He clung to Kade's side and Sophie's hand, refusing to let go of either. As Davey's temporary guardian, Kade filled out the appropriate paperwork with the boy clinging to him like a dog tick.

What would the little guy do if Kade didn't file for guardianship? Who would be there to hold Davey when he was scared?

Over Davey's head, he questioned Sophie with worried eyes.

"Everything will work out," she said softly and patted Davey's back. Kade wished he believed her. Experience had taught him exactly the opposite.

When a scrub-clad nurse called Davey's name, the trio followed her down an immaculate, antiseptic-scented hallway where Davey was readied for the procedure.

He looked small and scared in the hospital gown. When a nurse came at him with an IV, he screamed, but only breath emerged, a pitifully inadequate sound that left his body rigid and damp with perspiration.

Sophie soothed him as best she could, but in the end, the adults betrayed the child by holding him down. Davey fought, his chest heaving until he realized his struggles were in vain. Then he went limp and lay still and helpless. Kade's stomach hurt to look at him.

"You're okay, buddy," he kept murmuring against Davey's ear. "This is the worst of it." He hoped he wasn't lying.

A tear trickled from Davey to Kade, hot and condemning.

Kade squeezed his eyes tight and tried not to remember other children being hurt by adults. This was for Davey's good, not for bad.

But the parallels haunted him just the same.

"Almost done, Davey," Sophie said. She stood on the other side of Davey's head, smoothing the fine, pale hair from his brow. "You're such a brave boy. I'm proud of you."

When the trauma and tears passed and Davey was being wheeled away, Sophie accompanied the gurney down the hallway, murmuring her motherly endearments while holding Davey's pale hand until the very last moment. The sight chipped a piece off Kade's composure.

"We're doing the right thing," he told her when she returned, her smoky eyes glistening with tears.

"I know," she said. "But he doesn't."

Kade pulled her against his chest to both give and take comfort. After a bit, regrettably, she drew back and sniffled.

"Where's your Suzy Snowflake smile?" he teased gently.

Her lips wobbled upward in effort. He was tempted to kiss her then and there.

"Come on, I'll buy you some coffee," he said. "I you promise not to do the yogurt trick."

That was enough to bring a real smile. "If you're trying to make me feel better, you're succeeding."

Funny how happy that made him.

One cup turned to two and, just when he wa ready to beg a nurse for a glass of milk or a spoon of antacid to toss on the volcano, a door swung open and the doctor appeared.

Sophie grabbed for Kade's hand. Like any parent of a sick child—even though they weren't—they eagerly awaited the verdict.

After a quick introduction, Dr. Swimmer said "Well, folks, I have good news. Great news, actually. Davey's muteness is caused by a posterior glottic web."

"I've never heard of that," Sophie said.

"It's very rare, rarer still not to be diagnosed before this age, though I've read his records and understand the unusual circumstances."

"What is it? Can you repair it? Will he ever speak?"

The doctor smiled at Sophie's gush of questions. "A glottic web, in his case, is congenital. He was born with a webbing of fibrous tissue in his larynx, or voice box. His is so severe that the vocal cords are impeded. So he can't speak. Usually a child with this condition has breathing difficulties, too."

"He snores like a hog," Kade said.

The doctor inclined his head, smiling slightly. "I'm not surprised. His snoring is probably a stridor coming through the constricted tissues."

Medical jargon was lost on Kade. All he wanted to know was "Can you fix him?"

"We can."

A delighted gasp escaped Sophie. "That's wonderful news."

"I agree." The doctor fiddled with the flat surgical mask still tied around his neck. "But there's one problem. This isn't usually something I discuss with patients, but it's Christmas and Davey is a special case."

"Yes, he is," Sophie said. "Very special."

"Davey is not in any distress, so the surgery to repair his glottis web is elective. I'm willing to reduce my fee, but there are still hospital costs to consider, and according to his records Davey has no insurance and no family."

Kade got the message. "How expensive is this procedure?"

The surgeon gave them an estimate that sent Mt. Vesuvius into eruption stage.

Kade tightened his hands into fists.

Money stood between Davey and his voice.

Sophie was never short on hope. Kade may act as if the end had come, but she refused to believe it.

"We will not give up," she told him later that evening when they were alone at her house, Davey safely sleeping off his trying day under the careful watch of Ida June. "We can't."

They were seated in her living room, a domino game spread on the coffee table. The smell of hot buttered popcorn filled the house and warmed them.

Kade clicked a blank-four onto the board. No points. "Got a wad of money in your Christmas stocking?"

"Maybe." When he lifted one eyebrow, she played a two-six. "Ten points." She marked a giant X on the score sheet under her name. "My class will donate our cookie money."

Kade studied the board and his dominoes, finger and thumb stroking his bottom lip. "Noble, but nowhere near enough."

She knew he'd say that. She'd thought the same at first mention of the expense involved. But if she lived her faith, and she certainly tried to, she had to believe that nothing was impossible with God. "We'll make more. I also plan to hassle social services."

"Christmas is nearly over." With a sly grin, he

plopped down a domino and cried, "Give me fifteen, Miss B."

"Cops are so sneaky," she said mildly, marking his score. "You distracted me."

"Narc's are the worst." He leaned across the table and kissed her. "Now we're even. I'm distracted, too."

Sophie's lips tingled. She touched them. "Double distracted."

"What say we go for triple?" He leaned forward as if to kiss her again. She poked a piece of popcorn into his mouth.

"Foiled." He leaned back, smiling broadly, something he did more and more. When they'd first met, she'd wondered about his dark, broody personality, his lack of joy. Now she saw beneath, through the darkness to the incredible, sensitive man. The cynicism was a protective shell covering a tender heart. Sophie still wondered what he needed protecting from. Certainly not from her, and he'd opened his heart to Davey.

The thought of Davey brought her back to the problem of money. "People eat cookies year-round. If we have to we can bake and sell until the money is raised for Davey's surgery, no matter how long it takes." She slapped down a domino, her mind far from the game. "I believe in miracles, Kade, and Davey needs one. He deserves to have a voice like

anyone else, the sooner the better. Why not wish fo
a Christmas miracle?"

"You're something, Sophie," Kade said, thrilling
her to the bones. "I almost believe you'll make i
happen."

And then he slapped down a domino, chuckled
madly and said, "Twenty points."

The conversation with Kade played in Sophie'
head days later when a sad Davey sat at the round
table in the back of her classroom listlessly drawing
red circles on green construction paper.

He had these moments often since the funeral, a
sad, cold, painfully short event. Howard Prichard
had enlisted the services of a grief counselor bu
without a voice, Davey could only express his hur
with gestures and pictures.

The other students rallied around, trying to chee
the usually happy boy. Bless his precious soul, he
tried, but his heart wasn't in playing. He was sad
and hurt and orphaned. More than ever, Sophie
prayed for God to give him a miracle. She prayed
about a family, too, wondering as she had a dozen
times if she should adopt him. She was thinking
about it, long and hard.

Yesterday, she'd discussed the possibility with
Dad. True to form, he'd supported her all the way
Still, parenting required more than giving a child
clothes, food and a house to live in. A boy needed a

father, too, especially a boy like Davey who'd never had one.

She typed in the final edit of a note to parents. The back of her shoulders ached with unusual tension. As much as she loved Christmas, the last days of school before Christmas break were one of a teacher's greatest challenges. Kids, wired up with too much candy and the excitement of presents, vibrated the building with their energy. Add the concerns over Davey and she was tense.

She was glad when her charges headed to the gym for P.E. During this, her prep hour, she printed the note. In it, she'd explained Davey's situation and hoped to gain support for an ongoing cookie project.

Her students had wholeheartedly voted to donate the money to fund Davey's surgery. No surprise there. The trouble was, the budget was still several thousand dollars short. They had to make more.

She clicked her instant message, the principal's preferred method of interschool communication, and typed, Are you available for conference?

I have a few minutes. Come to my office, Biff typed in return.

Sophie rubbed the back of her head where a painful pulse throbbed. She didn't love the idea of discussing an ongoing cookie project with Biff. He'd been prickly since the encounter with Kade over the wassail bowl, but his approval was essential.

The bells on her doorknob jingled as she hurried

out and down the hall. For once she didn't stop to admire the silver-and-green garland looped across the hall or the cotton-ball Santas decorating the walls.

She strode into Biff's office and told him her plans.

"I sent you an email this morning, Sophie. Didn't you get it?"

She blinked. His wasn't the response she'd hoped for. "I haven't had time to check. What was it about?"

"We've decided to discontinue the fifth-grade fundraiser after today." His gaze held hers, firm and unyielding.

Sophie's heart sank into her empty stomach. The pulse in the back of her head thudded louder. "Won't you at least let me explain why we should continue?"

"This shouldn't come as a surprise, considering the conversations we've had on the topic. The project is discontinued, Sophie, and this subject is closed." He scribbled something on a pad of paper. Sophie had the insane desire to yank the pen from his fingers and bop him with it. "Furthermore, this is the last day you can tutor Davey Stephens in your class. He is not a fifth grader, nor are you a special-needs teacher. Mrs. Jacobs in the resource room will take over from here."

The words were a slap in the face. He was intentionally trying to upset her. "Why are you doing this? You know I'm a good teacher and my students perform well academically. Having Davey in our classroom has never interfered with that. On the contrary, my students have learned a great deal from the situation. You also know how important that little boy is to me. He just buried his mother!"

Biff flinched but did not relent. "I must do what's best for the students of Redemption Elementary."

"We're in total agreement on that. What we don't agree on is the method. Isn't there something I can do to change your mind? At least about the project?"

His nostrils flared. Whatever she'd done infuriated him. But what? Why wouldn't he tell her?

Surely, *surely,* his actions today were not personal. Were they?

With a flash of intuition, she asked, "Is this about my relationship with Kade?"

A vein flexed in his neck. He leveled her with a glare. "Don't be ridiculous. Now if you'll excuse me, I have a school to run."

He swiveled away to the computer at his side, leaving her staring at the side of his head in disbelief.

Whatever his reasons, Biff had just taken away her favorite project. With it went the money needed to give Davey a voice.

Chapter Fourteen

He had to cheer them up.

The thought was laughable to Kade, a man whose dark, depressed moods had given him an ulcer and sent him to a shrink.

But this afternoon, he felt like Mr. Happy Face compared to Davey and Sophie. As she did every day, Sophie brought Davey home from school. Unlike normal days, she rang the doorbell and when Kade had answered, his heart thumping happy thoughts at seeing her, she'd barely said a word.

He'd never seen Sophie down. It scared him. What would the world do without Sophie's sunshine? What would *he* do without it?

"Talk to me," he said, snagging her coat-encased arm when she started to turn away and head for her car. "What's going on?"

He sounded like his psychiatrist.

She pivoted back toward him and without a word, walked into his arms.

Endorphins flooded his brain. He could handle this.

He stroked her silky hair, let himself have the pleasure of a deep inhale of coconut-scented Sophie and warmed her with his body. Okay, and he might have kissed the side of her head. And maybe her ear.

She shivered. He drew her into the narrow entry and kicked the door closed, still holding her. A man would be crazier than he already was to let go now.

From the corner of his eye, he spotted Davey and Sheba flopped on Ida June's braided rug. They weren't wrestling. Davey wasn't giggling. Sheba's gaze looked soulful.

"Tell me who to beat up," he murmured. "Resolve my anger issues for a good cause."

She lightened some and sighed. "You would, wouldn't you?"

"Love to. Say the word."

"Maybe later."

Her response tickled him. "There's always hope."

"That's the problem. There isn't anymore."

The statement, especially coming from her, bewildered him. The trickle of fear pushed at his nerve endings. If Sophie lost hope, they were doomed. *He* was doomed. "What are you saying?"

She told him. Old stuff-shirt Gruber had put an

end to her hopes of raising Davey's surgical fee through the school.

"Why?" he asked.

She shrugged, pulling back from him. Much as he wanted her in his arms, he also wanted to see her face. That beautiful, sweet, loving face.

"Why doesn't matter," she said.

"Matters to me."

"I don't know what to do now." She gnawed her bottom lip. Such a waste of lips, he thought and touched his to the spot. Her lips curled upward and the relief that slammed him was like a tidal wave. He'd made Sophie smile.

"I'll kiss you forever if you'll be happy. Or I'll beat up Gruber. Either works for me."

The smile widened. "Silly."

Feeling better, though he'd accomplished nothing but a smile, he took her hand and tugged her toward the kitchen. "Stay," he said simply. "We'll figure this out."

Her answer was to sit down at the metal table. "There has to be a way."

He winked. "That's my girl. Miss Suzy Snowflake does not let bad news stop her."

He poured them each a glass of orange juice and left a third in the fridge for Davey.

"Doesn't the acid bother you?" she asked.

"Seeing you upset bothers me more." He took a sip, waiting for the burn. "Know what I think?"

"Most of the time, no." Lips curving over the edge of the glass, she sipped her juice.

"Forget old Biff," he said, suddenly struck with zeal and maybe a little revenge on the stuffy principal. "We'll continue the cookie project outside of school, only on a grander scale." He didn't know where the idea came from, but he ran with it. "Involve your church, the town, your friends."

"Kade!" Sophie sat up straighter. "That's a fabulous idea. This town knows how to work together. We do it all the time. I'm so used to doing this project on my own, I couldn't think outside the box."

His whole life was outside the box. "Put ads in the paper, posters up, send out eblasts."

"Wait, wait, wait. I have an idea, too." She bounced up and down, nearly levitating with excitement. "A cookie walk."

"Sounds perfect." He was clueless. "What is it?"

"We'll enlist the aid of everyone who's willing to bake cookies. Then instead of door-to-door selling the way we did at school, we'll ask the church to let us use the fellowship hall for a cookie walk. Customers will come to us. We'll set up tables, provide boxes and let customers choose their own cookies. Then we weigh the boxes and charge by the pound or the dozen or whatever."

Kade raised his hand in a high five. Her skin met his in a quick slap.

"We're going to get that Christmas miracle, Kade," she said with excitement. "I just know it."

He wasn't sure what he'd gotten himself into, but he'd succeeded in giving Sophie hope. And he felt like a million bucks.

Three days before Christmas, they were on a roll. Sophie had faith they could reach their goal during the holidays when people were more apt to give and more likely to need lots of cookies. If they didn't, she wouldn't be upset. They'd just keep trying. What she loved was that *Kade* had come up with the idea. *Kade* had told her to never give up.

That afternoon, she and Kade took Davey to the mall to shop for gifts, sat him on Santa's lap even though he might be too old and paid too much money for a photo taken by a teenage girl in an elf costume. Kade grumbled about commercialism and ordered extras.

If she'd not been in love with Kade before, she was now. From the moment they'd formulated the plan, he'd shifted into high gear. Ads appeared in papers, the fellowship hall was booked and cookie bakers signed up for shifts to create mouthwatering delights.

Davey, who'd been told that he could have a voice, was suddenly himself again and excited to the point of drawing pictures of a blond boy with music flowing from his mouth. Kade was teaching him a simple song on the guitar, and the notion of a singing Davey clutched at Sophie's heart.

Hope was everywhere. Especially inside Sophie B.

Two days before Christmas, a coffee klatch of sassy seniors crowded into Ida June's kitchen to teach the youngsters a thing or two about cookie creation. Three ladies argued over recipes for the world's finest raspberry thumbs while doting on Davey and bossing Kade around. The males, badly outnumbered, sneaked freshly baked samples and grinned when a gnarly finger was shaken in their faces.

"You have green frosting on your chin," Kade said, pointing to Davey. The boy smiled, teeth as green as grass.

"He's eating up all the profits," Ida June said and shoved another cookie at him. "Gluttonous child."

Sophie traded laughing glances with Kade. Excited about the fundraiser, about Christmas, about the services at church, about the scary joy of falling in love, tonight she was excited about something else, too.

"You also have frosting on your chin," Kade said to her. "Red."

She swiped futilely at her face. "Where?"

He moved closer, eyes dancing with mischief. "Looks delicious. Shall I?"

"Kade," she warned, sidestepping. As much as she enjoyed flirting and teasing with Kade, she didn't want to give the sassy seniors anything to talk about.

"Oh, Sophie, quit playing hard to get." Ida June flapped her oven glove. "The two of you go somewhere else to play kissy kissy. This kitchen is too small for courtin' lovers."

Sophie was sure her face turned redder than the raspberry jelly. "Ida June!"

"Go on, get out of here."

Three other sassy seniors grinned in speculative delight.

Kade grabbed her hand. "Escape while we can."

Fanning her cheeks with one hand, she let him drag her out of the too-hot kitchen into the backyard. The cool air felt wonderful. Sheba came along, equally eager to escape the heat and noise.

"That was embarrassing."

"No," he said, moving in. "This would have been embarrassing." He kissed the frosting from her chin.

Sophie hugged him, happier than she could remember. Being with Kade filled the empty spaces inside her. Did he, she wondered, feel the same?

"This is the best Christmas." She rested her head on Kade's chest and listened to the steady heartbeat. Dependable. Strong. Like him.

"Close," he said.

She tilted her face to his. "So you *are* doing Christmas?"

"Don't get pushy." But the words were light and

easing. They gave her new hope that the man she loved could be the man she'd always dreamed of. She yearned to admit her love and hear his reaction, but something held her back.

Please, Lord, she thought. He's come so far and he's such a good man. Heal his heart completely.

"You need a coat," he said.

Sophie was tempted to say he could keep her warm. Instead, she said, "I have something exciting to share."

He tilted back, eyebrows raised. "You won a million and Davey's surgery is paid for."

"Sounds good, but no, although this has to do with Davey."

"Okay."

"I talked to the social worker today."

"And?"

She took a deep breath, both excited and scared. "Someone wants to adopt Davey."

The earth shifted beneath Kade's feet. He didn't know whether to shout hurrah or kick something. He'd been giving some thought to adoption himself, not that he could pass muster, considering he was seeing a shrink. Anyway, he didn't figure they'd let a nutcase like him take on a kid.

"Kade?" Sophie's voice intruded. "Did you hear me?"

He cleared his throat, shaky inside as if his vol-

cano had erupted and caused an earthquake. "Th
family better be a good one. I'm going to chec
them out. Not just anyone can have him."

She smiled a little. "I feel exactly the same, bi
this is not a family per se. It's a woman. A singl
woman." She held her arms out to each side. "M
I'm applying to adopt Davey."

His heart shifted into arrhythmia, bounding an
pounding as if adrenaline shot through every cel
Sophie was adopting Davey? This was good new
Great news actually.

Then why did he feel as if she'd kicked him in th
gut?

Needing to regain his bearings, he stepped bac
to watch Sheba scare a bird from the fence. Th
was stupid. He should be jubilant.

"He's a lucky kid."

Really lucky. Stupid of him to feel left out. Bi
they'd been a team, a trio of him and her and th
quiet little boy. Hadn't they?

Where did he fit in? He scoffed, facing the fact
He didn't.

"I've been praying about it for a while—"

She had? Why hadn't she told him?

"And counseling with Dad and my pastor. Dave
likes me and I adore him. He's adjusted to school.
can do this. I want to."

He touched her arm. "You don't have to convin

ne, Sophie. You'll be fantastic. You already are. Just vhat he needs."

They'd discussed the boy's future a dozen times. "hey'd shared their hopes for the right family to ome along. Had she ever mentioned adopting him? 3y herself?

Mentally, he kicked himself. Why should she tell im anything? He was nothing to her. They'd been hrown into this bizarre situation by chance because hey both happened to be near a certain Dumpster t the same time.

Just because he'd fallen in love with her didn't 1ean she returned the feelings.

But she did. He knew she did. And the best thing e could do was wish her happiness and get out of er life. He told himself that every day. And every ight, he vowed to move on. Then morning dawned nd like an addict, he sought her out because she 1ade him feel human again.

Now he could let go. He had to. He could go back o Chicago comforted knowing Sophie and Davey ad each other. They'd be happy and loved and safe ere in Redemption.

Sheba barked at something in the corner of the ard. Kade grabbed the sound as an excuse.

"Better check on Sheba," he said, and walked way from the finest woman he'd ever met.

Man, he needed to call his shrink.

* * *

Inside Ida June's overheated, overcrowded kitche
Sophie boxed cookies and pondered Kade's reactior
to her announcement. He'd said all the right words
but she had a hard time believing he meant them.

"What are you so quiet about?" Ida June askec
elbowing Sophie to one side to take another cartor
from the yard-high stack. "My nephew do some
thing he shouldn't? I'll box his ears."

Sophie shook her head. What could she answer
Even she didn't understand what had just happenec
When he'd walked off toward Sheba, she'd followec
Part of her wanted to ask what was wrong, but he'
pretended everything was the same.

It wasn't. Even though she couldn't put her finge
on any one thing, she felt a change in him.

They'd made small talk until her teeth started t
chatter. As if a strange tension hadn't risen betwee
them, Kade had taken her hand and they'd gon
inside.

"Just tired," she told Ida June.

Kade took the packed box from her. "Go. We'
finish this."

His gentle, solicitous gesture both confused an
touched her. She had the weirdest urge to cry.

With a deep dread in her chest, she studied hi
beloved face and prayed to understand him better

"Okay," she said. "I want to tell Davey tomorrov
Will you help me explain?"

An odd expression crossed his face, but he re-
lied, "You know I will."

He followed her to the entryway and helped her
nto her coat.

"Kade," she said, screwing up her courage, "is
omething wrong? Did I say something to upset
ou?"

Out of sight of the sassy seniors, he leaned in and
issed her forehead in a long, lingering, almost sad
iss.

"Sophie," he said, taking both her hands in his so
hat they formed a bridge between them, "I've never
let anyone like you. You're amazing."

Her heart clattered in her chest. "I feel the same
bout you."

"Shh." He shook his head to stop her from talk-
ig. "Not true. You don't even know me. Not really.
just want you to know, when I leave this town, I'll
ever forget you. If you ever need anything, call me.
nd no matter what I have to do, Davey will get that
urgery."

Shock waves prickled the hair on Sophie's scalp.
Now she understood his odd behavior. He was
eaving and hadn't known how to tell her. "But it's
hristmas. You can't leave now."

*You can't leave ever. My heart will break. I love
ou. Please don't go.*

But she didn't say any of that. Playing the drama
ueen would only embarrass them both. Kade had

never said he was staying in Redemption, and apparently she wasn't enough to keep him here. Kad was going back to Chicago and to whatever ha ripped him in two.

Chapter Fifteen

Christmas Eve dawned with bright white skies threatening a snow. Throughout the day meteorologists, with *The Nutcracker* music playing in the background, built up expectations of a white Christmas.

Darkness came early this time of year, and by nightfall a few flurries swirled.

"Spittin' snow," Ida June said when Sophie and her dad picked up Davey for candlelight service. "It won't last."

Sophie hoped she was wrong. A white Christmas sounded lovely to her, especially this year when she could use the extra punch of Christmas spirit.

"Is Davey ready?" she asked.

Smiling shyly, the towheaded boy appeared behind Ida June dressed in a dark suit and tie.

"Oh, my, who is this handsome young man?" Sophie leaned in for a hug." A whisper of Kade's cologne on Davey's skin struck her with longing "And he smells good, too." She straightened, but Kade's scent followed, taunting her. "Thank you for getting him ready, Ida June, and for the suit. That was thoughtful."

"Not me. Kade." Kade again. Sophie fought off the ache. For all her noble talk about loving without expecting anything in return, she'd wanted things to turn out differently.

With her usual bluntness, Ida June tugged a stocking hat over Davey's ears and asked, "What's going on with you and my nephew?"

The truth came easy. "Nothing."

Ida June snorted and rolled her eyes. "Don't spit on my back and tell me it's raining, girl. Give me a little credit for having a brain. Kade's started that roamin' again."

Sophie tugged at her black gloves, instantly concerned. "Roaming? I don't know what you mean."

"Can't sleep. Just like when he first got here. He was doing better for a while and now he's roaming around at night again like some kind of hoot owl. He drives that wild car of his, goes out to the river, walks the yard. He's gonna catch his death if he keeps it up." She sniffed, snappy glare accusing. "I thought you'd fixed him."

Sophie couldn't fix what she didn't understand. "He said he's returning to Chicago soon."

"Told me that, too." She looked back over one

shoulder and raised her voice. "I think he's full of baloney, going back there when everything he wants is here. That place nearly killed him the first time around."

If Kade was within hearing range, he'd know Ida June's opinion.

Although amused by the other woman's antics, Sophie had circled this mountain too many times. She didn't know what had happened in Chicago and apparently Kade never intended to share. "He's a grown man."

Ida June grunted. "Didn't know there was such a thing."

The silly statement brought a small smile to Sophie's lips, though she remained adamant. The ball was in Kade's court. She'd done all she could.

Except tell him the truth, a small voice whispered. That she loved him. She'd miss him. She needed him. But Kade had enough stress. She wouldn't weigh him down with guilt over her.

"We have to run, Ida June," she said, touching a hand to the older woman's arm. "The invitation to come with us is still open."

"No, you go on. Mildred Phipps is coming by." She yanked the front door open. A car chugged slowly past on the damp street. Disappointingly, the snow had stopped. "Tell me one thing, though. Do you care that my nephew's leaving?"

"Yes, I do," Sophie answered softly. "Very much."

"I thought so." Ida June smacked a fist into her palm. "The way of a fool is right in his own eyes, but a wise man listens to advice. I'm thinking my nephew needs some sound advice. Right upside his hard head."

Sophie leaned in and hugged Kade's aunt. If advice would break through Kade's wall, he would be the one adopting Davey and he would never mention going back to Chicago. "We'll have Davey home early, but we might stop for ice cream."

Ida June waved her off. "I'm not worried. At least not about Davey. Now go on before you let out all the heat."

The past two days had been harder than Sophie had imagined. Kade was still in Redemption, but he'd distanced himself. She saw him, talked to him, and every time she did, she prayed that whatever drove him would be resolved. Even if he was never hers, she wanted him to be happy and at peace. Ida June's comments had confirmed he was neither of those.

Soft voices and a friendly reverence greeted them inside the foyer of Redemption Fellowship. Piano music floated from the sanctuary on the tune of "Oh, Little Town of Bethlehem."

The church was beautiful this time of year with huge wreaths hung along the sides of the sanctuary and lush green garland tied with red bows looped across the front. In one corner, a glorious ceiling-high tree glittered with angels and stars. Over the carved crèche Sophie had loved since childhood, a banner heralded Light of the World. This year, local wood craftsman Jace Carter had painstakingly restored the figures to their splendor as a gift to the church where he and wife, Kitty, had been married last summer.

Sophie waved at familiar faces as she herded Davey toward a pew with her father right behind. Along the way, an usher distributed thin white candles cupped with drip protectors.

"We'll light this later," she said to Davey's curious, upturned face. The poor lamb had limited experience with church, but he was well-behaved and interested. His mother, despite her emotional fears, had taught him many good attributes. "Don't worry, Grandpa and I will help you. You won't get burned."

Sophie's dad beamed at the new title she'd bestowed upon him. Davey, too, seemed thrilled to have a grandparent, something he'd never had.

"About time I got to be a grandpa," her dad had said when she'd announced her decision to adopt Davey. She'd sought his wisdom and prayers, knowing Davey would need a male role model. As much as the child admired Kade, his hero wouldn't be here.

If she let herself, she'd worry about how Davey

would take the news of Kade's departure. He'd had enough losses.

Dad had mentioned as much when she'd told him of Kade's decision to return to Chicago. He knew she, too, was hurting and the protective father in him wanted to make things better for both her and Davey.

Sophie wished he could. But they'd long ago discussed the chance that Kade might not love her the way she loved him, and she clung to Dad's mantra: love was always worth the risk.

Now the new grandpa placed a loving hand on Davey's shoulder and guided him into the pew. Both her men looked so handsome, Sophie's heart swelled with pride and love.

"Is that a new suit, Dad?" she asked, shucking her coat.

"It is. Is that a new dress?"

Sophie laughed and smoothed the hem of the red asymmetrical sheath. The tiny beading on the edges winked beneath the lights. "Dad, I've worn this on Christmas Eve for the last three years."

"You're so beautiful, you make it look new."

Sophie never doubted that he meant every word. Dad didn't see an ordinary, simple schoolteacher who barely wore makeup. He saw a beauty queen. "Thanks, Daddy. I love you."

"Ditto." He squeezed her hand, his gaze searching her face. "You okay?"

"Sure." A little sad perhaps, but Dad knew. She wished Kade was with them on this special night, not only because she loved him, but also because he needed the peace and healing found in God. "I have a lot to be thankful for."

"We both do. A new start, a new family, a son for you and a grandson for me. Pretty nice Christmas gifts." Her dad winked down at Davey. "Christmas is about a child, you know. Davey brings fresh meaning to that."

Yes, Christmas was about a child with no place to lay his head and no home to call his own.

Sophie slipped an arm around Davey's shoulders and squeezed gently. The same had been true for Davey, but not anymore. The Lord had sent him to exactly the right place to find a new family to cherish him.

"I love you, Davey," she whispered. He grinned his crooked grin and nodded. He knew she loved him and he enjoyed hearing it. What would it be like to hear him say those words to her?

Oh, how she prayed for Davey's Christmas miracle.

The piano rendition of "Oh, Holy Night" grew more subtle and Pastor Parker stepped into the pulpit to begin service. With quiet demeanor the blond pastor spoke briefly of the long-ago night when God's love came down to earth and became the light that still shines in a dark world.

When time came to light the candles, the sanctuary went dark except for the star shining over the crèche. A lovely, peaceful reverence filled Sophie's spirit as she lit her candle from her father's and they both shared the flame with a little mute boy. This was the way it would be, her father's eyes told her. As a family, they would raise Davey in the light of God's grace.

With flames flickering and "Silent Night" swelling with glorious beauty, Sophie prayed for the future. She prayed for Davey's miracle. She prayed for Kade, and as she did, she released him and her love for him to God the way her father had released her mother.

"Heal his heart, Lord," she whispered into the candlelit shadows. "Heal his spirit and his soul, and wherever he is, let him feel your love on this most holy night."

A wellspring of peace flooded her being.

God would go with Kade. And so would her love.

When the service ended the trio started out of the church, moving slowly through the hushed crowd. No one spoke much, and she could see the service had blessed others as it had blessed her.

Her father gently caught her elbow. With a jerk of his head, he motioned toward the far corner of the church.

Sophie's heart leaped. She fought down the joyful cry that shot into her throat.

Kade sat alone on the very last pew. Elbows on his knees, eyes closed and forehead propped on clasped hands, he didn't look up even though people moved past him toward the exits.

Sophie turned a questioning look toward her father. He shrugged and shook his head. He didn't know how long Kade had been there, either.

"I'll take Davey home," he said quietly. "I think you're needed here."

Yes, she was sure of it. Kade had come at her invitation and he needed her. Even if they didn't say a word, he needed to know she was here…and that she cared.

She spoke to Davey, gave him a hug and promised to see him tomorrow on Christmas Day. Her soon-to-be son left eagerly when her dad offered a stop at the ice-cream parlor for mint chocolate chip, his favorite.

Pulse hammering in her throat, Sophie made her way toward the man who held her heart. He looked lonely and forlorn sitting there, but she was ecstatic to see him.

Without a word, she slid into the pew next to him. He didn't acknowledge her presence, so she waited, praying silently for wisdom and guidance but mostly for him to find whatever it was he needed.

After a while, without looking her way, he slid

his hand to hers and squeezed. His fingers trembled, and Sophie ached for him.

"I never thought I'd ever come inside a church again," he said quietly, as if to himself.

"Why?" she murmured, pulse thudding in her ears. *Help me, Lord, to say the right things.*

Kade drew in a deep breath and exhaled on a gusty sigh. "Some bad things happened. I lost confidence in God. Maybe I was even angry at Him, which is pretty stupid on my part."

"He's a big God. He can handle it."

He turned his head toward her then, those beloved dark eyes full of sorrow. "*I* couldn't."

"What happened?" There. She'd asked. He could tell or not, but at least she'd made the effort.

"I worked undercover narcotics. Special task forces."

"You told me."

"Yeah." He pulled her hand onto his knee and massaged her fingers as if the contact eased him. "I'm not sure I can tell you the rest."

"Nothing you say will change the way I feel about you."

He gazed at her with a question in his eyes but didn't ask. She hoped he could read the love she beamed his way.

"You sure?" he asked.

"Positive. Please tell me what hurt you so badly, Kade. Tell me why you turned away from the Lord."

He tilted his head to stare up at the ceiling and sighed again. "My aunt said you'd feel that way. She also said I needed to find God again, but I wouldn't find him roamin' around like a hoot owl."

Sophie chuckled softly. She couldn't help herself. The feisty old lady had followed through with her threat to knock some sense into her nephew's head. "I love that spunky woman."

For the first time, Kade's face lightened. "Me, too." He recaptured her fingers and said, "I've been sitting here since the second hymn following her advice, asking God to help me."

"And?"

"I thought He'd let me down. Bad things happened to kids and He didn't stop them. I think I get now. He hated what happened as much as I did."

Kids being harmed? The concept prickled the air on Sophie's scalp. "I thought you were a *drug* agent."

"I was, but the job went deeper than anyone expected. The drug cartel had branched out." He closed his eyes, swallowed and said, "Into human trafficking."

Sophie's heart stopped beating for a nanosecond. Horror gripped her. "Oh, no. Not children."

"Yes." The grip on her fingers tightened to the unbearable stage. "I reported it to my superiors. They told me to take it deeper, find the source." His lips curled. "Being a good team player I did as

I was told, and all the while kids were being use
in unspeakable ways." He shook his head. "I don
want to tell you."

"Don't, please. I understand enough." Enough t
know what had driven him to the edge. A man c
compassion who harbored a guardian's soul, Kad
would break at not protecting a child.

"I knew. And I did nothing but gather evidence.
He scoffed, self-loathing thick around him.

She shuddered to imagine the horrors he'd likel
witnessed. How did a person ever cleanse suc
images from his mind? "Did you make any arrests?

"Oh, yeah, we got our bad guys. They're awai
ing trial in a cushy prison, but the arrests can't eras
what happened to those kids. They'll carry thos
scars for the rest of their lives."

The implication sickened Sophie. Her stomac
roiled. If Kade struggled at remembering, how muc
greater was the burden on a child?

"I hate myself for that, Sophie," he went on. "
should have done something to save them. The
were helpless kids. I should have stopped it."

"Could you have? Think before you answe
Kade. I don't know a lot about drug cartels b
enough to know they are powerful. Could you hav
stood against all of them? Wouldn't you have ende
up dead? And then the criminals would never hav
been stopped. You might not have saved some, b
you ended the cycle and saved others in the future

"You sound like my shrink." When she tilted her head in question, he said wryly, "Told you I'm a nutcase."

"Nothing wrong with seeing a doctor if he's helping you."

"He might if I talked to him more."

"I know another physician you can talk to. No charge." She smiled softly. "The Great Physician."

"Yeah." He nodded, mouth in a soft line of agreement. "That's what I've been doing tonight."

"And?" she urged softly.

"I don't want to go back to Chicago."

Adrenaline shot through Sophie's bloodstream. She sat up straighter, almost afraid to believe the implication. "You don't?"

"I left my soul in Chicago. I found it again in Redemption. I also found something else."

"What's that?"

He shifted on the padded pew and tapped his chest. "My heart."

Sophie thought *her* heart might jump right out to meet his. "I love you, Kade."

He closed his eyes and was quiet for a moment while Sophie's blood raced and her nerve endings jittered. Even if he didn't love her in return, she could go on with her life content and full. Kade had found himself again. He was on the road to recovery and peace.

When he opened his eyes, Kade said, "You blow

me away, Sophie. I'm hard and cynical. And I'v
done and seen things I won't ever tell you about
I don't understand why or how you can love me.
don't deserve you or your amazing love. But you—
he shook his head as if bewildered "—you deserv
everything."

"I have everything I want and need," she said
"Everything but you."

He tugged her closer, caressing her face with hi
fingers and his gaze. She felt his love long befor
he said the words.

"Then if you really want me, I'm yours. I lov
you, Sophie B. I'd be a fool not to." His lips curved
"And we know what Ida June has to say abou
fools."

Sophie returned his smile, the swell of joy a pow
erful thing.

The scent of candle smoke still lingered in th
church and the pastor had long since dimmed th
lights. She could hear him moving around some
where in the back, a wise shepherd who knew whe
to make himself scarce. He would wait, she knev
as long as necessary. He was, like his Savior, a goo
shepherd.

In the front of the church, the spotlighted crèch
stood out against a dark backdrop. She felt a righ
ness in declaring her love here in the church wit
the greatest love of all symbolized in a carve
wooden figure asleep in a manger.

Heart full to overflowing, she stood, drawing Kade up with her. "It's Christmas Eve. We should go and let the pastor get home to his family."

"Yeah, I have a stocking to fill myself." A full-blown smile spread across Kade's face as he took her hand. "Or maybe two."

Chapter Sixteen

Christmas morning dawned cold and clear. The snow, as Ida June predicted, had been nothing but a wish and a flurry.

Kade could have cared less. He'd slept fitfully but not because of his troubled soul. Rather, he'd been excited about the new beginning and he'd lain awake dreaming of a future with Sophie.

At six he rose, jittery for the day to begin. Sheba padded in, stretched her long, golden body and shook loose the remains of a solid eight hours. Kade let her out and back in, a fast trip thanks to the chill in the air.

Ida June would roll her eyes at his sentiment, but for Sophie's and Davey's pleasure, Kade tuned the radio to nonstop Christmas music. With a cup of his favorite caffeinated pain in hand, he plugged in the Christmas tree and slipped a few extra gifts beneath.

He loved that tree. Mostly because he loved the

woman who'd decorated it. He'd groused about the smelly little pine when Sophie had dragged him off to a tree farm, but he'd secretly been pleased. The tree had never been the problem. He had. He just hadn't believed he could deserve a Christmas with all the joy and love and trimmings.

Weird how messed up a man could get.

At seven, Davey, rubbing his eyes, stumbled into the living room in his blue-and-red superhero pajamas. His shaggy hair stuck up in a dozen places. He looked around, dazed and delighted by the pile of gifts and the bulging stockings.

"Place looks different, huh, buddy?" Kade leaned in for a hug.

Davey nodded, pointing toward the Christmas tree.

"Get dressed first. Sophie will be here soon." He checked his watch. "Very soon."

As Davey dashed away with Sheba close behind, the doorbell rang. Every nerve ending came to life. Who needed caffeine with Sophie around?

He yanked the door open. She'd come. She was here. Last night in the church had really happened.

She walked into his arms.

He enfolded her, basking in the feel and scent and essence of his woman.

She loved him.

"It wasn't a dream." He nuzzled her ear.

"If it was," she said, a smile in her voice, "we had the same one."

Content, he sighed against her coconut-scented hair. "You still love me this morning?"

"More."

He thrilled at her warm lips against his jaw.

"Merry Christmas to me." He pushed her back a little to kiss her properly. "And to you."

A gagging sound came from behind them.

"Please," Ida June grumbled, "I haven't even had my coffee."

Kade whirled around and grabbed his aunt, smacking her cheek in a noisy kiss. The white bun atop her head wiggled. "Love you, too, Auntie."

She pinked up. "Well, look who's been in the eggnog."

"We have something to tell you," he said, ready to shout the good news from a frozen rooftop.

Blue eyes snapping back and forth between Kade and Sophie, his aunt declared, "'Love, and a cough cannot be hid.'" She smacked her lips in satisfaction. "I've been saving that one."

Grinning, holding hands, Kade and Sophie joined Davey, Sheba and Ida June in the living room and Christmas Day began.

With love in her eyes and enough joy in her heart to burst into a Hallelujah Chorus—which she did a couple of times—Sophie watched Kade hand ou

Christmas gifts. At some point, he'd done some serious shopping. Even though she and her father had bought Davey several gifts, Kade and Ida June had bought more. Within fifteen minutes, all four of them had a pile of gifts stacked in front of them.

"Are we going to open them or admire them?" Kade asked.

That was the only cue Davey needed. With little-boy greed, he ripped into the bright paper, flinging ribbons and wrappings all over the living room. Sheba sat at his side, amber eyes adoring her boy.

Kade abandoned his Santa post to sit by Sophie. "You're all the present I want."

"Me, too," she said, handing him one anyway while wishing she'd purchased something more personal than a pair of leather gloves. "I bought this before...well, before last night."

He opened it, declared them perfect like her and gave her his gift. The silver paper and royal-blue ribbon were stunning. "I love the wrapping paper."

"You'll laugh at my gift."

"No, I won't." She opened the package and... laughed. "Leather gloves! I love them."

"Great minds think alike," Ida June declared, wagging a similar pair. "I like mine, too."

Kade motioned toward the stack of mail she'd brought with her. "What's all this?"

"Christmas cards, I guess. They were in my mailbox this morning, so I grabbed them before

coming over. Some are for Davey. I thought he'
enjoy seeing his name on them."

"Mail doesn't run on Christmas." He gave th
stack a curious look.

"Neighbors, probably. Just dropped them in th
box. We do that sometimes." She took one up an
opened it. A check fell out.

Kade retrieved the slip of paper from the floo
"Look at this. A donation to help with Davey's su
gery."

"What a lovely gesture," she said, heart welling

"Open the rest."

"You don't think—" Sophie shook her head
"Surely not."

But she opened another. And then another
Some were from friends, others from companie
or churches or civic groups. Card after card cam
with a check or cash and a note wishing Davey
Merry Christmas and a vocal New Year.

By the time she opened the last card, tear
streaked down her cheeks. Davey, alarmed, rushe
to her side and patted her face. His eyes begged he
not to cry.

"She's okay, Davey," Kade said, clearing hi
throat more than once. "Women cry when they'r
happy."

Ida June shoved a tissue into her hand. "Qu
blubbering before I start."

Because Ida June had been sniffing and her eye

watering for the past five minutes, Sophie laughed through her tears. She nearly had her composure back when the doorbell rang.

"Probably Dad," she said. Ida June had invited him for Christmas dinner. "I'll let him in."

The woman at the door was vaguely familiar. "We heard about the little boy who needs an operation. This being Christmas and all, my husband and I wanted to do something." She handed Sophie a check and walked away.

Stunned, all Sophie could say was, "Thank you. Merry Christmas."

The car had no more than pulled out of the drive when another, and then another and another arrived, each one bringing a donation for "the little boy who can't talk."

Each time there was a lull in visitors—some familiar, others strangers who'd read about the need in the *Redemption Register*—Kade reported on the total.

As the donations continued, Sophie's tears of joy turned to astonished jubilation.

The stream of visitors slowed at noon. While all three males played with Davey's race-car track, Sophie helped Ida June prepare the meal. Once in a while Sophie pinched herself to see if today was really happening.

A shout of laughter had her looking into the living room. Sheba, sitting on her bottom next to Davey,

moved her head in circles to the motion of a ca
racing around the track.

The doorbell rang again. Drying her hands on
dish towel, she went to answer, still laughing at th
dog and the trio of males she loved best.

Sophie pulled open the door. "Biff!"

Before her next breath, Kade appeared at her side
He didn't say a word. He didn't have to, but he di
glower. Sophie knew how upset he'd been when Bif
had discontinued her cookie project. Upset for he
sake.

She reached for his hand and gave it a reassurin;
squeeze.

"I figured you'd be here when you weren't a
home." Her principal looked as stiff and uncom
fortable as she felt. Though bundled against the col
in a long, wool chesterfield, his head was bare, hi
ears red.

Considering the words they'd had the last day
of school, she couldn't imagine what he was doin;
here.

"Merry Christmas," she said, for lack of anythin;
to say. She refused to hold a grudge at any time, es
pecially Christmas. Biff Gruber was her principa
She *would* get along with him.

"And to you." Biff thrust an envelope into he
hands. "Some of us took up a collection for th
Stephens boy. We wanted to help."

Sophie required concerted effort not to drop he

aw and gape. Astonished but touched as well, she
said, "Thank you, Mr. Gruber. Really. This is very
thoughtful of all of you."

"Yes, well—" he gave a short nod "—Merry
Christmas." And he walked away, back stiff and
ears as red as Rudolph's nose.

Sophie closed the door and leaned her back
against the solid wood. "This is almost too much
to comprehend."

Kade moved into her space, his dark eyes alight.
"No, sweetheart," he said. "You asked for a miracle.
I think you got it."

Awed and touched, she opened the check and
started to cry.

As she wept tears of joy, Kade pulled her into his
arms and murmured his love over and over again.

A small body shouldered in between the adults.
They went to their knees to take him into the circle
of love as a golden dog and a grinning aunt looked
on.

The miracles had just begun. Not one but many.
Davey would get his voice. Kade had found his hope
again.

And all of them had found each other.

All because of a lost and lonely boy…

A Christmas child.

* * * * *

*Don't miss the next book
in RITA® Award–winning author
Linda Goodnight's miniseries,
REDEMPTION RIVER.
Look for THE LAST BRIDGE HOME
in February 2012 wherever
Love Inspired books are sold.*

Dear Reader,

Cookies are a major topic in *The Christmas Child* as well as around the Goodnight house! We love our cookies, especially chocolate chip, and have tried many variances on the old standby recipe. Here is one of our favorites, first discovered by my grand-daughter, Lexi. Yummy!

Lexi's Cookies

1 cup butter or stick margarine, softened
¾ cup brown sugar, packed
¾ cup granulated sugar
1 egg
2 ¼ cup all-purpose flour
½ teaspoon salt
1 teaspoon soda
½ to 1 cup chopped pecans
1 package semisweet chocolate chips (2 cups)

Directions:

Preheat oven to 375°.

Cream butter or margarine; add sugars and beat until light and fluffy. Beat in egg. Stir in flour, salt and soda until well blended. Mix in chocolate chips

and pecans. Drop by teaspoonfuls onto a greased o
sprayed cookie sheet. Bake for about 8–10 minutes

Until our next visit to Redemption, Merry Christ
mas and happy reading.

Linda Goodnight

QUESTIONS FOR DISCUSSION

1. This story took place in the fictional town of Redemption, Oklahoma. What stands out in your mind about the setting? In what way did the setting add to the mood and tone of the book?

2. Who were the main characters? Did you like them and feel sympathy for them? Discuss their issues. How would you have helped each one resolve their problems?

3. Describe some of the secondary characters. Which ones seemed the most real to you? Can you identify with any one of them? Why?

4. Kade struggled with self-loathing. Why? Was he justified in his feelings? What made him so cynical?

5. Because of the things that happened during his year undercover, Kade distanced himself from God. How did this affect his life? His relationships?

6. Discuss why denying emotions is a bad thing. Name several ways Kade was harmed by his own emotions.

7. Sophie is a strong, happy character, but like everyone, she has problems. What is her biggest unresolved issue? How does it affect her relationship with men?

8. What do you think about the way Sophie's father continued to love his ex-wife? Do you think he was right? Or just unwilling to move on?

9. Have you, like Kade, ever had a problem you felt you could not talk about? What happened? How did you deal with the feelings?

10. What is the primary theme of *The Christmas Child*? Can you give examples from the story to substantiate your answer?

11. Think about the title of this book, *The Christmas Child*. Who is this referring to? Is there more than one Christmas child in the story?

12. Sophie believes in miracles. Do you? Have you ever experienced a miracle? Describe it and how it came about.

13. Kade's personal motto is "Life is a rat race and the rats are winning." Do you have a motto? If not, can you think of one that fits your attitude and beliefs?

4. Christmas in Redemption receives major focus. What are your thoughts on town-sanctioned Nativity scenes?

5. Ida June and Popbottle Jones are considered too old to raise an adopted child. What are your thoughts on the topic of parental age and adoption? What about single-parent adoption?

LARGER-PRINT BOOKS!

GET 2 FREE
LARGER-PRINT NOVELS
PLUS 2 FREE
MYSTERY GIFTS

Love Inspired™

Larger-print novels are new available...

YES! Please send me 2 FREE LARGER-PRINT Love Inspired® novels and my 2 FREE mystery gifts (gifts are worth about $10). After receiving them, if I don't wish to receive any more books, I can return the shipping statement marked "cancel". If I don't cancel, I will receive 6 brand-new novels every month and be billed just $4.99 per book in the U.S. or $5.49 per book in Canada. That's a saving of at least 23% off the cover price. It's quite a bargain! Shipping and handling is just 50¢ per book in the U.S. and 75¢ per book in Canada.* I understand that accepting the 2 free books and gifts places me under no obligation to buy anything. I can always return a shipment and cancel at any time. Even if I never buy another book, the two free books and gifts are mine to keep forever.

122/322 IDN FEG3

Name _____ (PLEASE PRINT) _____

Address _____ Apt. # _____

City _____ State/Prov. _____ Zip/Postal Code _____

Signature (if under 18, a parent or guardian must sign) _____

Mail to the **Reader Service:**
IN U.S.A.: P.O. Box 1867, Buffalo, NY 14240-1867
IN CANADA: P.O. Box 609, Fort Erie, Ontario L2A 5X3

Not valid to current subscribers to Love Inspired Larger-Print books.

**Are you a current subscriber to Love Inspired books
and want to receive the larger-print edition?
Call 1-800-873-8635 or visit www.ReaderService.com.**

* Terms and prices subject to change without notice. Prices do not include applicable taxes. Sales tax applicable in N.Y. Canadian residents will be charged applicable taxes. Offer not valid in Quebec. This offer is limited to one order per household. All orders subject to credit approval. Credit or debit balances in a customer's account(s) may be offset by any other outstanding balance owed by or to the customer. Please allow 4 to 6 weeks for delivery. Offer available while quantities last.

Your Privacy—The Reader Service is committed to protecting your privacy. Our Privacy Policy is available online at www.ReaderService.com or upon request from the Reader Service.

We make a portion of our mailing list available to reputable third parties that offer products we believe may interest you. If you prefer that we not exchange your name with third parties, or if you wish to clarify or modify your communication preferences, please visit us at www.ReaderService.com/consumerschoice or write to us at Reader Service Preference Service, P.O. Box 9062, Buffalo, NY 14269. Include your complete name and address.

LILP11I

Love Inspired®

SUSPENSE

RIVETING INSPIRATIONAL ROMANCE

Watch for our series of edge-
of-your-seat suspense novels.
These contemporary tales
of intrigue and romance
feature Christian characters
facing challenges to their faith...
and their lives!

AVAILABLE IN REGULAR
& LARGER-PRINT FORMATS

For exciting stories that reflect traditional values,
visit:
www.ReaderService.com